The
Celtic
Horse

JOHNNY MEE

DEDICATION

To my family

OTHER BILLY MACK THRILLERS:

THE PERSIAN WALTZ
Volume 1 - Vienna

THE OTHER RULE
Volume 2 - London

THE CARDINAL RULE
Volume 3 – Rome

THE SWEETEST PAYBACK
Volume 4 – Barcelona

THE MONEY RULE
Volume 5 – Zürich

ACKNOWLEDGMENTS

Thank you:

Becky Goldberg for your great help with the story, your advice and editing.
Caroline Ciaglia for your story thoughts, insights and suggestions.
John Welsh for your story ideas and Ray Gunn.
Liz Scott for your marketing expertise and your encouragement.
Chris Kozak for your input and advice on the cover.

i

CHAPTER 1

Billy Mack rested his elbows on the bar, raised his right hand and wiggled his fingers. "Half pint of Guinness," he said.

"Half pint?" The bartender chuckled, jiggling his beer belly. The stout man had a rust colored crew cut with long sideburns. He studied Mack's face with a practiced look.

With a broad smile he added, "You must be a Yank."

Mack smiled letting him know he was right then said, "I have to keep my wits about me this afternoon."

The bartender rapped his knuckles on the old bar in agreement. He walked down the bar and grabbed a glass off a tray. He flipped it once then set the glass on a silver grate and began pulling on the tap above it.

Mack felt guilty sitting in a pub but he'd earned some alone time and a cool Guinness - even if only a half pint. He still had some work left to do. Before the sun came up, Mack had been busy trying to close a deal. He spent the morning shuttling between his lawyer's office and a conference room crowded with investors.

Pinning down big-money investors was like chasing chickens. After six exhausting hours, he succeeded to get each investor to sign on the bottom line. The only thing left was the money. Every investor assured him they'd have their funds transferred by end of day.

Mack looked around the empty, musty pub. The tables and chairs scattered around the room had seen better days. Mack turned his attention back to the bartender and silently watched the glass fill with soft brown liquid. When the glass reached three-quarters full, the bartender pushed back the tap and looked over at Mack. "We only pull proper pints at Mulligans. Or in your case, half pint."

"I've been told the most perfect pints... or half pints in Dublin are pulled at Mulligans," Mack replied.

"Not only Dublin," the bartender said with a nod, "but in all of Ireland, if I say so myself." He pulled the tap again and filled the glass to the brim. He carried it over to Mack like it held precious cargo. He gently placed it on a coaster in front of Mack and rapped his knuckles twice on the bar.

Mack raised his glass and said, "*sláinte*" (pronounced *slon-chuh*). He took a sip, smacked his lips and placed the glass back down on the bar. He studied his glass and asked, "Why does the Guinness taste so much better in Ireland?" He arched his eyebrows as he shifted his gaze back to the bartender.

The bartender's mouth hung open and his eyes bulged from their sockets. The blood drained from his face. He nodded feebly then turned and swiftly disappeared through the door leading to the back room.

Mack turned to his right and saw only empty tables. He swung back around left. On the barstool next to him sat a tall, desperately thin man wearing a faded green Notre Dame baseball cap pulled down low. The man raised the brim of his cap for Mack to see his emaciated face.

Mack's eyes widened. The man sitting on a stool that likely weighed more than him was a skeleton wrapped in a taut layer of skin. His eyes and cheeks were sunk deep against his skull and his skin defied color. His trench coat hung on him like it was draped over the back of a chair.

Mack tried to recover from his shock by nodding slowly and taking a sip from his glass.

The man waited until Mack looked back at him. He said, "I'm used to that reaction." He opened his coat wide enough for Mack to see the grip of a pistol in his shoulder holster. "That doesn't mean I won't use this." He paused. "Again."

Mack's jaw tightened as he raised his gaze to the man's face. He knew better than to say a word. When you're in a hole, don't dig.

The man said, "You're William McMillan but you go by Billy Mack. You and I are taking a walk. Let's go."

"I'm not going anywhere."

"I was willing to shoot the bartender if he didn't walk away. He did the right thing."

Mack looked down to see the man pointing a silver pistol at his chest.

"Move, before the police arrive."

"First, tell me why."

"We walk and talk."

The desperation and finality in the man's voice

prompted Mack to step off the stool. He slid a twenty Euro note under his glass, looked down at the pistol and said, "It's your dime."

"Smart choice," the man said. He let slip the trace of a smile as he slid the pistol back into its holster.

They walked out onto Poolbeg Street and turned right. The clouds were darker than when Mack walked into the pub. It felt like rain was coming.

At the end of the block, Mack heard sirens off in the distance. The man gestured for Mack to turn left.

They walked in silence until they reached a four-story gray stone building, a city block long. Two city buses were parked in front. Mack read the bus stop sign: Trinity College.

They walked on until the man pointed at a wooden door with an arched opening. "We're going in there." He tapped his coat above his shoulder holster. "I'm a desperate man with only one thing to live for so don't try me."

They came to a bench at the corner of a grassy square and sat. A group of young men with backpacks slung over their shoulders strolled by without noticing them.

The air felt heavy and the clouds grew darker. Mack held out his hand with his palm up, checking for rain. Feeling only the wind, he dropped his hand and said, "You have my full attention. What do you want with me?"

"I need your help." The man paused and looked up at the sky. "Notice I said *need* and not *want*? You know why?"

Mack shook his head.

He locked eyes with Mack and said, "I'm told you're the *one* man who can help me."

His words took Mack by surprise. He tried to read the man's gaunt, expressionless face. He finally said, "I have two questions for you. Why am I the *one* man? And who gave you my name?"

The man leaned forward and placed his elbows on his knees. He began speaking as if he were talking to the ground. "Not long after I married, my wife learned she could never have children. So when my wife gave birth to our daughter, she knew she'd given birth to a miracle. So did I. Then two years ago, my daughter, for her fourteen birthday went on a school trip to St. Petersburg. On that trip, she disappeared along with a classmate of hers. The Russian police investigated but never found a trace of either one and stopped working the case. My wife and I, together with the parents of the other girl, hired a private investigator to find them. Like the police, he came up empty. A year ago, we lost touch with the parents of the other girl. I assume they gave up."

The man looked over at Mack to see if he was listening. Mack, hanging on every word, nodded for him to continue.

"A short time later, my wife also gave up. When I left her alone for an afternoon, she lay on our daughter's bed and swallowed a handful of Oxycontin. In her note, she begged me to join her and our daughter but I knew in my heart our daughter was alive... is alive. I haven't been able to eat or sleep since." He looked at Mack with empty eyes. "I'm beginning to lose hope."

Mack averted his eyes and asked, "Why do you think I can help find your daughter?"

"Someone you know in Switzerland gave me your name. I'm to say hello from Caroline so that you'd know I'm on the level. You left quite an impression on her and her organization at *Kloster Einseideln*." He looked over at Mack to gage his reaction.

"Go on," Mack replied.

"According to her, you've had the misfortune of dealing with the man financing the Russian mafia's sex trade, a man named J Otis Weil. She also described him as a pedophile who prefers pretty young girls between the ages of fourteen and sixteen." He pulled a picture from his shirt pocket and handed it to Mack. "This was taken on her fourteenth birthday, the day she left for Russia."

Mack stared at the picture of a beautiful young girl in a plaid school uniform and white blouse.

Mack said, "From what I know about J Otis Weil, this is the type of girl he prefers. Once they reach seventeen or eighteen, he gets tired of them and sells them to sex traffickers and they disappear."

"Then you understand my urgency," the man said. "I've talked to anyone and everyone I thought could help. My last hope was Caroline and her organization. She said you and her worked together on a similar situation in Barcelona. Is that true?"

"Yes, with my niece," he said then corrected himself, "my adopted niece." Mack did not want to go into the details.

"So you understand what I'm going through. Does that mean you'll help me?"

Mack looked back down at the girl's picture uncertain if he could help or should help. There were too many unknowns. "How did you know I'd be in the pub?" He flicked his head in the direction they'd come from.

"I followed you from your lawyer's office. That's where Caroline said I'd find you."

That satisfied Mack the man was legit. Caroline would have already vetted the man before she gave him a scintilla of information. And he knew Caroline had the skills to track down anybody with just a few keystrokes. "What do you want from me?"

"I want J Otis Weil."

Mack mulled over his request then replied, "J Otis is an evil little man with no moral compass and rarely leaves Moscow so I can't promise anything."

Mack handed the picture back to the man. "I will talk to some people to see what can be done. First though, I have business deal to close this afternoon. That gets my full attention."

A spark of life ignited the man's bloodshot eyes. He handed Mack a card with only a phone number on it. "After two years, I can wait one more day. Call me once your business is completed. I don't sleep." He looked at

Mack like he was his Lord and Savior. "Thank you."

"I didn't get your name."

He wiped away a tear rolling down his bony cheek. "Waters, Nigel Waters."

"I'll call you tomorrow," he said.

Although Mack still had work to do to put the investment deal to bed, he knew the paperwork remaining was simple and routine. One thing though nagged at him. Paddy O'May, the genius inventor who every investor in the deal had bet big money on, was fragile and needed Mack's attention and encouragement, like a big brother watching over a little brother - at least until the deal was fully funded.

"I'll do what I can but I can't promise anything."

Waters nodded his understanding and walked away. By the time he passed through the arched wooden door he had new life in his step.

A light rain began to fall. Mack closed his eyes and wondered if it was a sign he'd given the man false hope?

§

CHAPTER 2

Later that afternoon

Paddy O'May listened to the jubilant buzz on other side of the heavy oak door while he nervously chewed on the nail of his little finger. A burst of laughter startled him and he pulled his finger away from his mouth. People on the other side of the door were having a good time. He debated his next move. The same debate he'd been engaged in most of his life.

Go in, don't go in.

He took a tentative step toward the door. He reached for the handle and his hand involuntarily jerked back. He stared blankly at the door handle. The debate returned.

Go in, don't go in.

He steeled himself. Part of him wanted to rush in and shout out the great news to the jubilant crowd. The other part of him screamed, *"Don't go through that door, there's a crowd of people in there... a crowd of people."*

He switched fingers and began chewing on the nail of his ring finger — or what was left of the bloody nub. Beads of sweat broke out on his upper lip.

He had to tell Billy Mack about the remarkable breakthrough with his invention or he'd burst. Even *he* barely believed the latest test results.

Paddy O'May stood five foot four and weighed seven stone *(98 pounds)* making him the textbook definition of a seven-stone weakling.

What Paddy O'May lacked in size he made up for with hard work and brains. Intellectually, he was a giant, often compared to Einstein, Edison or Tesla, sometimes all three at once. He thought outside the box, way outside the box and his mind never stopped working.

People who knew him admired his genius — a genius with a giant flaw. He suffered from a crippling case of *Enochlophobia*, fear of crowds. He preferred to live in his own world, a world where he interacted with only a few people, people who understood him. It's not that he didn't like people, he did. He just preferred his interactions with people to be one on one. That's why he spent most of his waking hours in his workshop, tinkering with his *outside-the-box* invention.

O'May looked down and checked his clothes. A delaying tactic he'd used all too often. He'd dressed in his Sunday best, a hunter green corduroy sport coat with yellow pinstripes and brown elbow patches. It was a half size too big. Under the sport coat he wore a dull white dress shirt with an orange and green tie. Dark brown polyester pants, a white belt and brown leather shoes rounded out his ensemble. He couldn't afford a fashion sense — that was about to change.

Paddy O'May *was* different. He thought different. He moved different. He even smiled different. His latest creation, an incredible invention, was beyond comprehension and it took a man like him, someone who thought different, who thought outside the box, to come up with the idea and make it work.

Paddy O'May was a self-taught engineer who defied the laws of physics. He proved the third law of physics: *For every action there is an equal and opposite reaction,* was wrong. He proved: *For every action there is also a greater reaction* — if the right elements are combined. After years of everyone doubting him, he began winning over the skeptics.

O'May's formal education ended on his thirteenth birthday, unlike the highly educated and wealthy crowd on the other side of that door, many of them his former skeptics.

He gazed down at the front of his well-worn sport coat. With his free hand nervously pulled at a loose thread then quickly realized he better leave it alone or his jacket might fall apart. He returned his focus to the door.

What do I do?

His feet remained stuck to the floor as the debate in his head returned.

Go in, don't go in.

The crowd on the other side of that door consisted of investors with advanced degrees and tons of money. They were there to get a piece of O'May's revolutionary invention, an invention that would turn the world upside down and radically upset the balance of power. The people in that room couldn't wait to throw money at

Paddy O'May, lots of money.

That's because the crowd on the other side of the door were in the business of making money. They knew that just being in that room and investing in Paddy O'May, in his invention and in his company, The Celtic Horse, they were certain to get filthy rich or, more properly, filthier rich.

O'May stared at the door trying to muster every ounce of courage he had in order to turn the handle and walk inside. He had to go inside that room and tell Billy Mack of the breakthrough in his invention. He stopped chewing on his fingernail and reached for the handle. For the umpteenth time he told himself his fear of crowds was irrational and to go ahead, turn the handle and walk inside.

Inside the large conference room, Billy Mack tried to focus on Paddy O'May and closing the deal to secure the funding for The Celtic Horse. His mind however, kept returning to Nigel Waters. He couldn't shake the image of a desperate man, a walking skeleton, from his mind.

He checked his watch and thought about sneaking out and finding O'May. It would take his mind off Waters. He decided to give himself five more minutes and then he'd make an excuse to leave.

Paddy O'May looked up and down the hall then reached for the door handle. When his hand touched the handle he jerked it back up and wiped the sweat from his upper lip. He decided he needed a running start.

Another delaying tactic.

He strolled away then turned on his heel, marched back to the door and turned the handle. He closed his eyes, pushed open the door and stepped inside.

He'd done it. Now all he had to do was open his eyes.

He reluctantly opened his eyes to see a crowd of well-dressed men and women milling about. He blinked a few times to adjust his eyes to the bright lights.

Most of the crowd filling the large conference room turned their heads and smiled widely at the rare sight of Paddy O'May, the reason they were all in that room.

At the far end of the room, running along the windows, stood a long wooden table surrounded by leather chairs. Most of the crowd hovered in small groups around the table. There were too many people for O'May to count.

His legs wobbled and he felt dizzy. He braced his right hand against the wall and desperately scanned the room for a friendly face.

Billy Mack, standing at the far end of the table, looked over. It surprised him to see Paddy O'May inside a crowded room. It also diverted his attention from Waters. He smiled, inspired at the sight of the man of the hour. As soon as O'May's hand hit the wall, Mack's smile disappeared.

"Keep it together, Paddy," he muttered.

Mack brushed back his thick brown hair and adjusted his tie as a delaying tactic. He couldn't rush over without bringing additional attention to O'May. He forced his smile back on his face and excused himself from the small group surrounding him.

He'd taken too long excusing himself. Gregorz Pogladek had already crossed the room and hovered over O'May. As he spoke, he wagged his finger up and down, a few inches in front of O'May's nose. At six feet tall, Pogladek, the Managing Partner of Falcon Investments, towered over O'May, obviously trying to intimidate him. His tailored suit, starched collar and diamond encrusted tie clip added to the pressure, as intended. O'May's head bobbed, nervously following Pogladek's pointed finger.

Mack didn't like what he saw. Even though Pogladek, the second largest investor in the room, putting seventy-five million dollars into The Celtic Horse, that didn't give him the right to intimidate O'May or even lecture him.

Mack quickened his pace, looking each person in the eye and nodding as he walked by. Everyone in the room was either an investor or part of an investment team and the last thing Mack needed was for everyone to see O'May being intimidated. Given O'May's fragile state in or around a crowd, a meltdown was highly likely.

What prompted O'May to come into a crowded room? The investment deal was going better than expected and Mack wanted to keep it that way.

He slowed as he neared O'May, listening intently, trying to pick up Pogladek's words.

Pogladek must have sensed Mack's presence and stopped wagging his finger. He patted O'May gently on his bicep. "We will talk later," he said as if O'May had no choice. He turned, nodded once to Mack and strolled away.

Mack waited for Pogladek to be well out of earshot

then said, "Paddy, what are you doing in here? We still have an hour or so before the wire transfers are done and the deal is officially closed. I thought you were staying in your workshop until the closing dinner."

Seeing Mack's friendly face relaxed O'May enough to release his grip on the wall. A small amount of excitement surfaced in his eyes.

"I have to tell you the news. It's unbelievable." O'May glanced over at the crowd and went back to chewing on the nail of his little finger. A thin layer of sweat returned to his upper lip.

He saw Mack staring at his finger. He dropped his hand and slipped it into his pocket then forced a smile.

"What is it you have to tell me?" Mack asked hoping to take O'May's mind off the crowd.

O'May surveyed the room. His voice stammered and cracked as he said, "Not... not.... in here."

§

CHAPTER 3

As the blood drain from O'May's face, Mack said, "Take a deep breath, Paddy. Let's go talk in the hall."

Mack peered nonchalantly around the crowded conference room to send a message. He put his arm around O'May's shoulder, more to hold him up than for comfort.

Mack led him out into the hall, leaving the door open so as not to raise any eyebrows. In case anyone was looking, Mack forced a confident, relaxed look to emerge on his face. He looked back inside for everyone to see.

With the crowd out of sight, the tension in O'May's body slowly dissipated. He was in a one-on-one situation, away from the dreaded crowd and back into his world. The color returned to his face.

"Before you tell me what you're so excited about, tell me what Pogladek wanted," Mack said.

"He wants me to reconsider and pledge the patents for my invention as collateral. It wasn't an *ask*. He insisted or he promised to find a way to get out of his investment."

"What did you tell him?"

"I said no and then I added that the patent wouldn't do any good without the detailed drawings, the schematics. He threatened to involve his lawyers."

"He's bluffing," Mack said.

"I thought so. That's why I told him he had to talk to you. Before he could respond, you showed up."

"Gregorz never gives up. I'll give him that." Mack said and stepped further away from the door. "Don't let him lecture you again. If he or anyone demands collateral, tell them the position of your company is that no equity investor, including me, gets collateral. If they argue, direct them to me or Steve Gray."

O'May dropped his chin as if to check if his fly was open. He blushed, even though his fly was closed. "I will."

Mack added, "You said the exact right thing, Paddy."

The relaxed look spreading over O'May's face comforted Mack. He said, "Now, Paddy, what is it you were so excited to tell me?" Mack spoke slowly, deliberately.

O'May perked up and excitedly shifted his feet. "I just finished another test run and hit fifteen hundred, again."

"What?" Mack replied. He instinctively turned to see if anyone heard what O'May said, a reflex that was second nature in his business. He glanced into the room then partially closed the door and walked further down the hall, followed closely by O'May.

He turned and faced O'May. "Are you certain?"

O'May entire body overflowed with excitement and he looked as if he'd grown a few inches.

"I finished another test run early this morning and triple checked the numbers. After what I saw, I'm confident we can go up to two thousand with some minor adjustments."

Mack steadied himself. In his first deal as a full partner, The Celtic Horse was proving to be an even greater invention and investment than he ever imagined.

"This is huge, right?" Mack said as if he needed to pinch himself.

O'May nodded and grinned proudly.

Mack scratched the side of his neck debating if he should go back inside and make the announcement to the entire group.

He studied O'May while he contemplated the incredible news and his next move. He fought a smile, a huge smile.

His decision was easy. The invention belonged to O'May and his company. Any news like this big must come from him. He patted O'May on the shoulder and said, "Tonight at the closing dinner, I want you to make the announcement. It will be the cherry on top of the sundae."

O'May didn't react the way Mack expected. Instead, he peered down at his shoes like a child just given a timeout.

"Why the long face, Paddy? This is great news."

"There is no way I can speak in public. I just can't..." O'May's voice trailed off.

At hearing the exciting news Mack had forgotten

about O'May's crippling phobia. He exhaled then calmly said, "No worries, Pius can make the announcement." Pius Malloy was O'May's business partner.

O'May's long face lingered.

"Smile, Paddy. All is good in the world and it's only going to get better."

"I haven't told you everything. Shortly after I finished the test run, officials from the American Internal Revenue Service showed up at the workshop asking questions about the prototype. I refused to answer any of their questions. That's when they demanded I give them the technology."

"The IRS?" Mack asked. "Why would the IRS come to Dublin? More importantly, why do they want the technology?"

"They gave a rambling answer about replacing lost revenue."

Something didn't smell right to Mack. He held his hand up before O'May said another word. "How many were there and did they have an appointment? Is so, why wasn't —"

O'May interrupted Mack, saying, "There were three, two big brutish men and a thin, sharply dressed man. The sharply dressed guy was definitely in charge because he hung back while the two big guys peppered me with questions.

"I told them to make an appointment if they wanted to talk to me. They said the Internal Revenue Service doesn't make appointments because it gives people time to destroy incriminating evidence, whatever that means. Then, they went back to firing off questions, ignoring what I'd just said."

"What questions?"

O'May thought for a second. "They started off asking specific questions on how the prototype worked. I told them the Celtic Horse was still in the final stage of development and then my excitement got the best of me and I let slip about the new test results and given the progress, the prototype should be ready for production next week. They wanted copies of the technology, specifically the detailed drawings. I asked them why they needed the drawings. They made the same vague remark about figuring out the tax basis. I made it clear that even if I had them with me, they would never get them. They became very upset. After that, they walked over to the thin guy and huddled together for about ten minutes. The skinny guy strolled over and asked lots of questions about you. He seemed to know everything about you."

"This man knew everything about me? What did he ask?"

When Mack played third base for the Chicago White Sox, he was considered the best curveball hitter in baseball because he could see a curve coming from the time it left the pitchers hand. But this was a curve he didn't see coming. He knew nobody at the IRS.

"He wanted to know your connection to The Celtic Horse, the name of your hotel, where you were during the day, if you had a car or driver, things like that. I said today wasn't my day to watch you. He didn't like that and let me know it. He flicked his fingers and the big guys hurried back over. I thought they were going to kill me but they both just stood over me. They were clearly sending a message. The boss snapped his fingers and one of the brutes said they would be in touch and they left. I didn't like the way he said, '*be in touch*.'"

"They of course gave you their business cards when they left?" Mack said sarcastically.

O'May looked confused as he shook his head.

For a second, Mack wondered if the thin man was Nigel Waters. He quickly dismissed it. Waters showed up at the pub alone and he certainly wasn't sharply dressed.

Mack thought about asking O'May to describe the thin man when the door behind Mack creaked open. Mack turned to see a smartly dressed woman standing in the doorway. He studied her in silence. Her slender face accentuated her long neck. Dangling from her ears were shiny silver earrings in the form of tiny handcuffs. Her light brown hair had sunny streaks of blonde and was cut short on the sides. The hair on top was longer and tussled, like she'd just climbed out of bed and ran her hand through it. She never took her brown eyes off Mack, staring him down.

For a moment, Mack felt ill at ease but couldn't look away. Her eyes told him not to.

She surprised Mack by coming up to him and sticking out her hand. He realized he'd been giving her the once over and immediately regretted it. He hesitated before taking her slender hand.

Her eyes then smiled as she held Mack's hand. She was no stranger to getting the slow once-over. "My name is Anna Swerdlov, a Principal with Falcon Investments. I recently joined Gregorz Pogladek's team. It's nice to meet you, Mr. McMillan, or I should say, Billy Mack."

She leaned to her right, looked past Mack and said, "You're Mr. O'May, the reason we are all here, right?"

O'May nodded, worried more people would come out into the hallway and join them.

Swerdlov stepped closer to Mack. He sensed she was about to assert control. He'd seen this move more times than he cared to remember in deal negotiations.

Her jaw tightened for a nano-second then eased. "You and I need to talk about working together... after tonight's closing dinner, of course."

Mack was taken aback by her... *chutzpa* — he couldn't think of a better word to describe it. It compelled him to look her in the eye and deliberately hold her gaze.

"You're rather direct," he said.

"I go after what I want and I get it."

At least she's honest, Mack thought. Unable to read her face and body language, he said, "We'll cross the working-together bridge when we come to it." He pointed over to O'May and said, "For now, let Paddy and me finish up here?"

Swerdlov furrowed her brow as if she suspected foul play. Then she stroked Mack's forearm and gave him a look that said, '*I understand.*'

She turned to go, stopped and looked over her

shoulder. "You'd better hurry. An issue is percolating with a couple of investors and it may develop into a problem for our deal. If it happens, those investors might walk away or force the money they agreed to invest to be delayed." She raised her eyebrow and held up her long, sinewy finger. "But you didn't hear that from me."

Seeing the surprise on Mack's face, she added, "If you need me, you know where to find me."

Mack and O'May watched her stroll back into the conference room.

When she melted into the crowd, O'May asked, "What does she mean about investor problems, Billy?" His voice was weak and his upper lip quivered.

Mack shrugged, "That's the first I've heard about it. Let's go see what's up."

O'May turned so white you could show a movie on his face.

"You worry too much," Mack said with a tight smile. He patted O'May on the shoulder. "Everything will be fine, Paddy. Go back to your workshop. I'll call you when it's time to celebrate at the closing dinner."

The worried look on O'May's face bothered Mack. He may be a genius but he's a fragile genius.

"The one thing we asked of you is for you to be at the closing dinner. It's important you be there, Paddy... as you agreed."

O'May meandered away chewing doggedly on his ring finger.

§

CHAPTER 4

For the next hour, Mack worked the crowded conference room carefully conversing with people trying to decipher which investor was liable to cause a problem.

In every deal Mack closed, there were always one or two investors demanding last minute changes or *deal creep,* causing headaches and threatening to walk away if their demands weren't met. Mack always listened respectively and when they finished, thanked them for considering the deal, wished them well and then walked them to the door. He never once gave in to their demands and no investor ever walked out the door. He was prepared to do that again to anyone in the room.

Confident he'd talked to everyone he considered a potential problem, he strolled over to an empty space by the wall and perused the room looking for Anna

Swerdlov. She was nowhere to be found. If she was warning him about an investor problem, why wasn't she in the room? Was she up to something?

Mack's attention shifted to the only person not participating the festive banter dominating the room. Off to Mack's left, Steve Gray sat at the head of the large conference table with a pile of papers in front of him. Gray was the attorney tasked with drafting the documents and confirming the transfers of money to The Celtic Horse. Gray represented Mack's Chicago-based investment company, Baxter, Israel & Gunn, or BIG as it was known on Wall Street. BIG was the lead investor in The Celtic Horse financing. Gray's job was to close the deal while at the same time protecting BIG and its partners, including its newest partner, William A. McMillan, or Billy Mack, the man leading the deal.

Mack wore the only suit he owned, a navy blue *Joseph Abboud* bought at a going-out-of-business sale in Chicago. He only wore a suit and tie when he attended a deal closing and always the same suit with a white shirt and one of two green and gold striped ties.

Mack strolled over to Gray. "Everything on track, Steve?" he asked.

"I made a few corrections in the company's off-shore incorporation, nits and nats, nothing significant. The document packages will be delivered within the next fifteen minutes and the first tranche of funds is expected to be available. I should have everything wrapped up before the closing dinner."

"Before we do that, let me run something past you that may significantly affect the deal," Mack said.

Gray cautiously set his red pen on the table and massaged his lips together. He crossed his arms and gave Mack his full attention. This meant if Gray didn't like what Mack said, he'd stare at him until Mack grew visibly uncomfortable then give him a lecture on deal creep. It was a feeling Mack had experienced more than once.

"Start running." Gray was a man of few words.

"What?" Mack asked, not understanding Gray. His mind battled between the good news about O'May's invention, Swerdlov's investor warning and the persistent image in his head of Nigel Waters, the walking dead.

Gray replied, "You *wanted* to *run* something past me that could affect the deal."

Mack came back to the here and now and lowered his voice so only Gray could hear him. "Paddy informed me he finished another test run and confirmed the prototype hit fifteen hundred."

Gray relaxed. "That's good, right?"

"Very good."

"What's your question?"

"Should we announce it to the investors before the monies are transferred into the company's account?"

Gray closed his eyes and rubbed his chin in thought. After a few deliberate seconds, he opened his eyes, removed his glasses and cleaned them with his tie.

"This means the investors are getting a much better deal than originally valued, right?"

Mack nodded.

"Are you planning on reducing the investors ownership percentages based on these new results and the company's increased value?"

Mack didn't have to think about it. "No, we have a signed agreement. When we valued the company, Paddy, Pius and I had a conversation about the possibility of an increased valuation. We agreed to keep our word with investors."

"Then make the announcement at the closing dinner. You'll be heroes," Gray said decisively and turned his attention back to the documents.

"That's why you get the big bucks, Steve."

Gray lowered his head to hide his grin. He straightened the pile of papers and went back to reviewing the documents.

Mack thought of telling Gray about the rumor of investor problems then thought better of it. Instead, he ambled over to a group of investors and stood quietly. They were too excited to notice him.

He fixed his attention back on the room hoping to spot Anna Swerdlov.

§

Mack thoughts drifted back to Swerdlov's comments about a potential investor problem. At least it pushed Nigel Waters' image from his mind.

He masked his anxiety and peered around the room looking for her. Where the hell was she? When his eyes reached the corner of the room, he spied Pius Malloy standing alone near the back exit. Malloy and O'May co-founded of The Celtic Horse.

Pius Malloy leaned against the wall with a satisfied grin on his face and a half-pint of Guinness in his hand. His title was Chief Executive Officer but he and Malloy ran the business together. No decisions were made without the approval of both men.

At five-foot-five, Malloy was an inch taller than O'May. Like O'May, he was thin but with the early onset of a potbelly. His ears stuck out a little too far and his receding hairline stretched across the top of his head. He wore a tired gray suit, blue shirt and an orange and black tie that hurt the eye if you looked at it directly. Malloy had no illusions of being a Cary Grant type. He made up for that with his quick wit, easy smile and razor sharp intellect.

Mack liked the fact that neither Malloy nor O'May cared how they dressed. He knew they didn't have much choice. Both men sunk every penny they could beg, borrow or scrounge into keeping The Celtic Horse afloat as they built their prototype. O'May invented while Malloy ran the day-to-day business. They were a good team.

Mack waved at Malloy and gestured for him to come over.

Malloy placed his glass of Guinness on the windowsill and meandered through the crowd, nodding politely as he passed by. Confident he knew why Mack had waved him over and wasn't about to stop and engage in conversation.

Approaching Mack, he said, "You confirmed the wire transfers and the money is in our account, right?" He stood triumphantly, unable to hide his delight.

"Not yet," Mack replied and looked at his watch. "I expect the first tranche to be funded before the closing dinner. That being said, I need you to make certain Paddy is at the dinner and on time."

Malloy's posture deflated. He didn't relish chasing after his partner. He pulled out his phone and tapped the screen. Bringing the phone up to his ear, he said, "Paddy's probably in his workshop."

Mack thought about asking Malloy if he knew about O'May's breakthrough in the latest test run. He decided not to mention it. If Malloy hadn't yet heard, the good news should come directly from his partner.

Malloy lowered the phone from his ear with a concerned look on his face. "That's very strange, Paddy didn't answer. He always answers my calls... even if he's in the loo."

Mack glanced at his watch. There wasn't much time

before the closing dinner. He looked at Malloy afraid to ask his question. He grimaced. "Can you go find him?"

Malloy was determined to remain in the room. He began to argue, thought better of it and perused the room. He waved at Kieran Sweeney, the company's Chief Financial Officer and gestured for him to come over.

Sweeney was tall, thin and loped when he walked. Although Sweeney had only been at the company a short time, he knew Malloy wanted him to go look for Paddy O'May... again.

"Have you seen Paddy?" Malloy asked.

Sweeney sighed and said, "I saw him this morning in his workshop. He was rechecking his numbers on the latest test run of the prototype. Why do you ask?"

"I can't get ahold of him," Malloy replied.

Sweeney rolled his eyes. "He knows what time he needs to be here. I reminded him of it more than once this morning."

"I saw him about an hour ago," Mack said. "He came by after-" Mack nearly let the latest test result slip. He cleared his throat. "After he met with two officials from the American Internal Revenue Service."

Sweeney shot Mack a strange look. "He met with American revenue officials? Why were they here and why wasn't I involved in the meeting? I'm the CFO and I deal with all tax matters."

Mack always made it a point to avoid wading into corporate turf battles. When pulled in to those battles, he knew to choose his words carefully.

Before Mack put in his two cents, Malloy said, "I'm not surprised, Kieran. Before you joined, we received a number of written inquiries from the American Internal Revenue Service. They want to go over the power source to learn how to calculate the excise taxes."

"We can worry about this later," Mack said. "Someone needs to find Paddy and get him here on time."

"Go find Paddy, will ya, Kieran," Malloy asked.

"Jeasus, that muppet is always gone at the wrong times," Sweeney mumbled. He strode away shaking his head, annoyed he had to go look for O'May... again.

Malloy walked a few steps behind Sweeney then veered off to chat with a small group of investors standing near a side table.

Watching Sweeney slip out the door, Mack couldn't

help but grin sympathetically.

For the next thirty minutes, Mack worked the room singling out investors he'd not previously spoken with, trying to determine if any of them could spell trouble. He made it a point to tell each and every investor the deal was done, the documents were signed and their funding was expected to be in the company's account by end of day, as agreed in writing.

After speaking with the investment group from Vienna, Mack perused the room and noticed Steve Gray had organized the documents in a row running down the conference table. He ambled down the table marking off a checklist on a pad of paper. This meant Gray's work was done and the money was about to fill the coffers of The Celtic Horse. The only task left was to get Paddy O'May to the closing — no easy feat.

Mack strolled over to Gray. "I see we're done."

"That's why you pay me the big bucks," Gray replied, keeping his focus on the row of documents lying on the table.

Mack felt a light touch on his left shoulder and turned.

Anna Swerdlov stood close to Mack. She grinned but it wasn't a friendly grin. "We have to talk." It wasn't a suggestion.

"Can it wait?" Mack asked. "The closing-" Mack stopped talking when he saw Kieran Sweeney march through the conference room door. Sweeney stopped and tried to hide whatever was bothering him. He was failing miserably.

Mack turned to Swerdlov and said, "Give me a few minutes."

He hurried over to Sweeney.

§

CHAPTER 5

The worried look on Sweeney's face intensified as Mack approached. When he reached Sweeney, the lanky Irishman turned his back on the crowd staring at him and lowered his chin. He whispered, "I can't find Paddy anywhere. I combed the entire bloody building, every nook and cranny. I even drove over and went inside his workshop, which is off limits. I turned both places upside down but no Paddy."

"Did you call his cellphone?" Mack asked.

The question surprised Sweeney. He shook his head and said, "Pius tried calling him so I didn't even think to."

"Stay here while I talk to your boss," Mack said. "In case someone asks about Paddy, say you last saw him in his workshop."

"That was this morning."

Mack knew he was treading on slippery ground. He knew that if O'May, the reason everyone was here, was missing he would have to inform the investors. But this wasn't the right time to say anything. Nobody knew for certain if anything was wrong. He patted Sweeney on the shoulder for reassurance and said, "No one can accuse you of lying."

Mack covertly signaled for Malloy to meet him over by the door.

Mack didn't like the sour look on Malloy's face. Malloy was anticipating bad news and investors were picking up on it as he walked through the room. The crowd began turning their attention to Malloy approaching Mack.

"Come with me, Pius We have a couple of last minute things to go over before..." Mack said loudly then let his voice trail off as he neared the door. Mack led Malloy out into the hall and away from the door.

As soon as they reached the hall, Malloy asked, "Where the hell is Paddy?"

Mack shrugged and said, "Kieran couldn't find him." He shot Malloy an uneasy look then turned and walked down the hall.

Malloy followed holding his phone in front of him, punching in O'May's number as he walked.

The distant ringing of a phone drifted in from down the hall. Mack marched toward the sound. Outside the men's bathroom, he stopped. The ringing came from behind the door.

Mack pushed open the door, took a step inside and asked, "Paddy, you in here?"

Mack's words echoed through the white-tiled room. An acrid whiff hung the air, waking up Mack's sniffer. It smelled like bad fruit.

Malloy followed Mack inside. He crinkled his nose and pointed to the wastebasket. "The ringing is coming from in there, Billy" he said, trying not to breathe.

Malloy reached in and pulled out the phone. It rang as he held it up for Mack to see. There were red splotches on the phone. He tapped the screen of his phone to end the call.

"What the hell?" Malloy said, unable to take his eyes off the blood on the phone.

Mack paid no attention to Malloy. He stared at a

smear of blood running down the wall beneath the paper towel dispenser. The streak intensified as it approached the floor and ended in a dark red Rorshach blot.

The bathroom door flew open.

Mack jumped back to avoid being hit by the door. The door caught Malloy's shoulder but he didn't feel it. He was engrossed in the bloody phone in his hand.

Kieran Sweeney stood in the doorway and surveyed the room. He sniffed and made a funny face.

Mack gathered himself and asked, "Did you check this room before, Kieran?"

"I opened the door and yelled for Paddy but there was no answer," Sweeney replied as he looked around the room.

Mack noticed something on the floor inside one of the stalls. He walked over, pushed open the stall door and braced. On the floor, partially hidden behind the toilet was a hunter green sport coat with yellow pinstripes and brown elbow patches. A splatter of dark red spots covered the right sleeve.

Malloy grabbed the coat from Mack. "That's Paddy's coat. It's the only sport coat he owns."

"Oh good Lord, no," Sweeney muttered under his breath after noticing the blood on the sport coat.

The three men heard a noise behind them and slowly turned. Anna Swerdlov stood just inside the door with her right hand buried inside her handbag as she glared at them with righteous indignation. She knew something was amiss.

A strained silence gripped the room.

Malloy took his eyes off O'May's sport coat and shifted them over to Swerdlov, her hand still inside her handbag. He began to hyperventilate.

Mack heard Malloy's gasps echo off the white tiled walls and realized he was starting to panic.

Worried Malloy may pass out, he put his hand on Malloy's shoulder then gently took the bloody phone from his hand and slid it into his pocket.

"Relax Pius," Mack whispered. "If she wanted us dead we'd have already met our maker." He hoped that would calm Malloy. It didn't.

Mack brought his attention back to Swerdlov, her hand still inside her handbag. He wondered if he'd just whispered wishful thinking to Malloy.

He braced as he decided his next move. Should he rush her before she had a chance to pull out her gun and get the draw on him? He slowly removed his hand off Malloy's shoulder and shifted his feet.

Swerdlov realized Mack and Malloy were staring at her hand hidden in her handbag and were deciding what to do. She let out an impertinent chuckle then calmly said, "I'm only taking out my phone." She slowly removed her hand, held up her cellphone and waved it like a white flag.

Malloy went back to breathing normally.

Everyone in the room looked over at the streak running down the wall and the bloody Rorshach blot on the floor.

A few seconds later, Swerdlov broke the silence. "That odor you smell is ether and if that blood belongs to who I think it does, someone should be calling the Guards (*Police*)."

Having seen one too many detective shows on TV, Malloy dropped O'May's coat and shivered. "Jeasus, I just contaminated the crime scene."

"Relax," Swerdlov said. "You did no such thing."

"We have to call the Guards right now," Sweeney said. He stared at Swerdlov's phone then raised his eyes to meet hers and realized she wasn't about to make the call.

Sweeney fished his phone from his front pocket and said, "I'll call the Guards." He sucked in a deep breath, tapped his phone screen while mumbling, "nine, nine, nine," loud enough for Swerdlov to hear. When she didn't react to his mocking tone, he stuck his phone in his ear and walked out. Mack, Malloy and Swerdlov followed.

Sweeney abruptly stopped and stammered into the phone. He caught himself and explained that his boss, Paddy O'May was missing. Blood and his coat were found in the office bathroom. When he hung up, he let out a sigh of relief and said, "The Guards are on their way."

"We can't let anyone into this bathroom until the police arrive," Mack said. "Somebody find a security guard... and hurry."

Sweeney loped down the hall, turned left and bounded down the stairs.

Malloy began to follow Sweeney then abruptly stopped in the middle of the hall and stared at his feet. He had no idea what to do.

Mack and Swerdlov looked at each other then over at Malloy. Unable to find the right words, Mack said, "This ain't good."

He and Swerdlov stood in awkward silence trying not to make eye contact.

When what he'd said hit him, Mack felt like a moron. He needed to say something more thoughtful than *this ain't good.*

"We can't think the worst," he added. "Perhaps Paddy slipped and fell and drove himself to the hospital? He's a very self-reliant man."

The way Swerdlov looked at him, Mack knew she didn't believe a word he'd said. She calmly replied, "Rather than assume anything, let's see what the Guards have to say." Swerdlov looked down at her phone.

Mack didn't like the expression on her face and quickly said, "Wait until the police get here before you call or tell anyone."

Swerdlov ignored Mack and studied her phone like she hadn't decided whom to call first. She took her attention off her phone when Sweeney and a burly security guard wearing a gray uniform shirt and black pants jogged over from the stairwell.

Sweeney gave the guard clear instructions not to let anyone in the bathroom until the police arrive then walked over to Malloy standing in the middle of the hallway and led him back toward the conference room.

"You don't want Malloy going into the conference room in his state," Swerdlov said. "Unless you want the deal to crater."

"Kieran," Mack yelled. "Take Pius to his office and stay there until I come for you."

Sweeney nodded and nudged Malloy to his left. He marched him away with his arm firmly around Malloy's shoulder.

Halfway down the hall, Malloy shook free, spun around and marched back to Mack. "If I'm not in that room it may raise questions we don't want to answer."

"There is still the lingering, or I should say, potential problem with one or two disgruntled investors and a missing management team won't help," Swerdlov said softly enough for only Mack to hear.

Mack waited until Malloy and Sweeney were inside the conference room. He turned to Swerdlov. "I don't give a damn about any disgruntled investor," he fumed. "All that matters is we find Paddy."

"We can't think the worst. I'm sure he's fine," she replied with no conviction.

§

CHAPTER 6

Mack and Swerdlov walked over to the conference room door and scrutinized the crowd inside. They both knew their body language needed to be reassuring. Mack stepped back from the doorway and asked, "Do you know Ray Gunn from my firm?"

"Of course. Everyone in our business knows him. He's a legend."

Mack pointed inside the conference room. "I need you to go in there and tell Ray I want to see him in private. It's important to make sure only he hears you. Can you do that?"

Swerdlov let out a soft laugh. "I promise not to make a scene. Stay here." Her eyes told Mack she didn't appreciate being talked down to like that.

Watching her amble through the conference room with every man stealing glances at her, Mack realized she was used to being the object of attention.

A couple minutes later, Swerdlov strolled back into the hallway followed by Ray Gunn.

Mack knew of Gunn's clandestine past and heard a few harrowing stories of his shadowy exploits from some shady or at least suspect people who worked with Gunn in his previous life. However, if Mack had to put his hand on the bible, he could only say the stories were rumors. At least he wanted to believe they were rumors.

Gunn's lips were pressed so tight together they were hermetically sealed. The look on his face told Mack he didn't like being pulled away from what he was doing or with whom he was speaking. Mack learned the hard way there was direct correlation between the tightness of Gunn's lips and his anger. Telling him about a missing Paddy O'May would not loosen his lips.

When Gunn saw Mack, his lips parted. He looked at Swerdlov with a hint of admiration. "Well done," he said. "You got me out here without telling me why. You've been well trained."

Swerdlov grinned proudly. She'd impressed the great Ray Gunn. She opened her mouth to speak.

Before Swerdlov could respond, Mack said, "We may have a problem, Ray. Paddy is missing and we found blood and his sport coat in the men's bathroom."

Gunn folded his arms across his chest. He stared off into nowhere. As was his habit before taking charge, he let his covert past, his experience resurface. It was a Catch-22: It felt good to have his old life back, it felt bad because of why it came back — something had gone awry and he had to fix it.

When confronted with a *situation*, Gunn learned to let his thoughts marinate before he spoke. He lowered his chin, studied Mack and then Swerdlov as if reading their minds.

After some deliberation, Gunn asked, "Besides you two, who else knows."

"Malloy and Sweeney," Mack replied.

Gunn looked around. "Where are they?"

"They're in the conference room over by the tea table," Swerdlov answered and raised her finger to indicate she had more to say. "From what I saw, they were working hard to avoid eye contact with the others in the room while trying to look calm." She added, "They were doing a rather *shite* job of it."

Gunn said, "Anna, go find them and bring them out here... with as few people as possible noticing?"

Swerdlov winked at Gunn and strolled back to the room.

Gunn let his arms drop. "Fill me in, Billy."

Mack rubbed his temples as he retraced his steps. He started his story at the point where he saw O'May walk into the conference room then grip the wall in panic. He covered O'May's brief conversation with Pogladek and the new test results from the last test run. The story ended with Sweeney calling the police.

When Mack finished, Swerdlov, Malloy and Sweeney were standing behind Gunn. Malloy and Sweeney looked like they were about to get sick.

Gunn strolled over and closed the conference room door.

"Kieran," Gunn said, his voice clear and firm, "when the police arrive, you stay with them. Show them the blood and the coat and do what you can to keep them away from the investors... for as long as you can. Billy and Pius, go back inside and mingle. Billy, confer with Steve Gray and have him come up with some plausible excuse to delay the closing dinner, if need be."

When the group began to move, Gunn held up his hands. "I'm not done." He waited for everyone's attention to come back on him.

"Not a word to anyone until we have more information."

As the group walked away, Gunn took Swerdlov by the elbow and said, "You and I should get some air."

§

Mack massaged his chin with his thumb and forefinger as he watched Swerdlov and Gunn walk away. He wondered where they could be going. He fished his phone out of his pocket and moved away from Malloy and Sweeney. He punched in an unlisted number of an unregistered business in Washington DC and waited.

"Mira Labs," a female voice said.

"Hi Adriana, it's Billy Mack. Is Nimesh in?"

"Hi Billy, I'll connect you."

After a series of clicks, a voice came over the phone.

"Hey Billy, it's Nimesh. If you're still in Dublin then this ain't no social call."

"I need a quick and dirty from you. Hopefully, more quick than dirty."

"Ask and you shall receive," Nimesh replied.

Mack lowered his voice. "After you did the background checks for me on Falcon Investments and Gregorz Pogladek, they added a new member to their team. Her name is Anna Swerdlov. Can you give me a high dive on her and if I need more, do a deeper dive?"

Mack listened while Nimesh typed furiously on his keyboard, quasi humming as he went. The typing ended but Nimesh's humming continued.

Thirty-seconds later, Nimesh said, "Anna Swerdlov joined Falcon Investments six months ago working out of their London office. I'm looking at a picture of her." Nimesh resumed humming. "I'll keep my frat boy thoughts to myself."

Mack grinned at Nimesh's comment. He knew exactly what Nimesh was thinking. "What's her story?"

"She graduated from London School of Economics two and a half years ago, top of her class. The only other reference is her job at Falcon. She joined the company three months ago."

"There's nothing for the two years in between?" Mack asked.

"Let me dig deeper. This may take a bit of time."

The typing resumed and Nimesh returned to his quasi humming.

A minute later, the typing ceased as did his humming.

"Anna Swerdlov was born in Belfast in Northern Ireland to an Irish mother and Russian father. Both were professors at Queens University Belfast."

Nimesh paused then murmured, "Oh my, how sad."

"Sad? What's sad?"

"Both her parents were killed in a hit-and-run car accident in Russia over a year ago. They were in the countryside outside St. Petersburg, apparently heading to the tiny town of Virki where her father grew up. According to the report, a very large vehicle, most likely a semi, ran a stop sign and T-boned their car. The truck driver simply drove away. There were no witnesses and the driver was never found."

"According to what report?"

"The report was written by the police department of the neighboring town of Tavry. The report is thin. I read you the entire accident report except for the make of her parent's car, a Lada." Nimesh huffed and said, "The communists made the Lada... that's a coffin on wheels."

Mack leaned against the wall. He felt sorry for Swerdlov, losing both parents at once.

"Anything else?"

"There's a younger sister, Alexa. Let me see... according to her birth certificate, she was also born in Belfast and recently turned sixteen."

"Does she live with Anna?"

"There's no mention. I'll dig deeper."

"While you're doing that, also look into what Anna did for the two years between school and Falcon Investments."

"I'm already on it. I call back once I fill in the blanks."

"Make it quick... please."

"How quick?"

"I need it yesterday, a man's life may depend on it."

"I hope it's not yours?"

"No, it's a man who needs to lead a long, healthy life."

§

CHAPTER 7

Back inside the crowded room, Mack waited until Pierre LeBeau, the chubby Managing Partner of the French Investment firm *Henri et LeBeau,* finished speaking with Steve Gray and walked away with a hangdog look on his face.

When LeBeau turned his head, Mack looked away but could feel LeBeau's eyes on him as he strolled over to Gray. He bent down and whispered, "Find a benign reason to delay the final documents for an hour or two."

He waited for Gray to look up then added, "I don't care what you come up with, just make it sound like a small glitch, a technical problem."

"We may have a good reason," Gray replied. "The French investors and the Maltese group, Falcon

Investments have come with a last second demand before they initiate wire transfers. I can use their deal creep as an excuse and it's legitimate."

"Good," Mack said, hearing but not realizing that Gray just informed him that some investors were actually throwing a wrench into the deal.

When Mack's mind caught up with Gray's words he bent down so he could whisper.

"What last minute demand?"

Gray leaned closer to Mack's ear. "Since they are the two largest investors after BIG, they want copies of the patent applications and the schematics... the technical drawings, the final versions. They also want the patents as collateral."

Mack looked around the room looking for the French and Maltese investor teams. For the first time in his career he welcomed deal creep.

He spotted Gregorz Pogladek, the managing partner of the Maltese group, Falcon Investments, holding court to an audience of a dozen people. As Pogladek spoke, he kept glancing back at Mack and Gray.

Mack leaned back down. "It's Pogladek who's making that demand. LeBeau doesn't have the *cojones* to go it alone."

"What do I tell him?" Gray asked.

Mack looked over at Pogladek giving himself time to think.

"Definitely a no go on the collateral, they're equity investors. No on the drawings as well. Tell them we'll provide copies of the schematics once we receive the certified documents from the patent office and that you'll need to draft an addendum to the agreements. That ought to satisfy them and we can use that as the excuse for the delay."

"What's the real reason for the delay?" Gray asked. His eyes told Mack that Gray knew this was more than a minor problem and he better be straight with him.

"Murphy's Law," Mack replied. He needed time to come up with the right words so as not to panic Gray.

Before he could tell Gray about O'May being missing, Malloy tapped him on the shoulder.

Mack turned to see Malloy's jaw locked tight and his cheeks dark red.

Behind Malloy, strutting across the room stood an impeccably dressed woman preening like a proud peacock fanning its feathers.

She marched straight up to Malloy and hovered a few inches over him.

Clearly surprised at her presence, Malloy said, "What are you doing here Claire?"

Claire Donovan removed her white shawl and handed it to Mack. "Be a dear," she said without taking her eyes off Malloy.

Mack reluctantly took the silk shawl and draped it over his arm.

Donovan kept her pompous grin on Malloy and said, "It's not everyday I get to see my brother become a millionaire." Before Malloy could answer, she turned to Mack and said, "Be a dear and get me a cup of Earl Gray with milk, not cream." She cavalierly flicked her hand toward the tea table by the far wall.

"Go, go."

"How much spit do you take your tea?" Mack replied with a venomous look on his face. He had no patience for people like her.

She glared at Mack, "Do you know who I am?"

"I haven't the foggiest."

"Then were on the same page. I have no idea who you are, not that *I* should."

Malloy cleared his throat and said, "Claire this is Billy Mack. We've mentioned him to you."

She looked at Mack and scoffed, "Oh, you're that once semi-famous American baseball player who now works for my brother." She huffed as she snatched her shawl from his arm and stormed across the room to the tea table.

"How can I put this, Pius? Your sister is Bi-" Mack bit his tongue, "an interesting specimen."

"She's not my sister. Her name is Claire Donovan. She's Paddy's older sister and a real pain in the arse."

That took Mack by surprise. "They're related? Who da thunk it? Paddy is so mild mannered, shy and reserved."

Malloy hesitated then said, "And she's the reason why. I avoid her every chance I get. That hasn't been easy and it's even harder since she found out about Paddy's invention and the amount of our company's upcoming investment."

"What's she doing here?"

"She's overly protective of Paddy, always has been. To answer your question as to why she's here, she's convinced she'll get a good chunk of Paddy's wealth once this deal closes."

Mack didn't know what to say. This wasn't the first time he'd witnessed family members latch on to a blood relative, or any relative, even distant relative about to become wealthy. Mack knew it was best to stay out of family business. What Paddy did with his money was his decision and his alone.

"She doesn't look like she needs the money. What does she do?"

"She owns the Irish rights to some anti-aging cream made from a combination of tiger urine and cobra venom that comes from Thailand or someplace near there. She also dabbles in real estate. Her husband is a commercial real estate developer. They drive matching silver Mercedes and preen like they're the toast of the town."

Mack peered over at Claire Donovan standing at the tea table. Pierre LeBeau was brewing a cup of tea for her. When he finished stirring he handed her the cup. She nodded then turned and strolled back over to Mack and Malloy.

Donovan took a sip of her tea and said, "Where's my

little genius? I want to congratulate him on this momentous event and help him celebrate."

Malloy tried to speak but no sound came out.

Mack rescued him. "He's finishing up a few things."

Donovan let out an exasperating sigh. "If I know Paddy, he's off hiding somewhere probably inventing something else and lost track of time. But I couldn't be prouder of him than I am right now." She turned, faced Malloy, happily nodded and said, "Have one of your people go find him... now."

"Excuse me," Mack snapped so forcefully that Malloy took an inadvertent step back. Donovan didn't flinch and glared at Mack.

Mack said, "Your brother will be here when he gets here and you know exactly why we only want him around a crowd of people for a short period of time and as short as possible."

Donovan smirked and said, "Then take me to him. At such a momentous time, he needs his big sister to watch over him."

Mack's experience in handling a demanding investor with unreasonable demands came in handy. He went with one of his standard lines, saying, "We need all hands on deck to make sure the documentation is complete and accurate. When it comes time for Paddy to be here, I'll get him here."

Donovan huffed. "Do you know who you're talking to? Not only am I the sister of the man who is changing this world, my husband is the leading real estate developer in Dublin if not in all of Ireland." She grinned proudly at Mack then at Malloy. "Now bring me to him."

Mack needed time to come up with a reason not to bring Donovan to see her brother. He held his hands up in mock surrender. "Fine, let me speak with the attorney in charge on a matter we need resolved then I'll meet you out in the hall."

Donovan whipped her shawl around her neck and victoriously marched out.

"Be careful with her, Billy," Malloy said so only Mack heard. "It's an understatement to say she's overbearing when it comes to Paddy."

Mack took a step then stopped. "Tell me something, Pius. If she is rich and powerful, why didn't she invest in her own brother's company? Especially when you were strapped for cash?"

"Her, her..." Malloy stammered then caught himself.

"Whenever we asked, she and her husband always said they were on the verge of closing another big deal and their money was tied up in escrow. We received the same excuse every time."

Mack thought about O'May approaching his own sister for money and instantly felt bad for him. It's no fun getting turned down by family when your back is against the wall. "How should I handle her?" Mack asked.

"Whatever you do, don't tell her Paddy is missing. She'll go ballistic and make a scene. I've seen her do it and it's ugly."

Hearing that, Mack dreaded facing Claire Donovan but knew it would be better not to delay the inevitable. He took a step toward the door and bumped into Pierre LeBeau, the French investor.

LeBeau held up his hands as if to apologize for running into Mack. "Billy," he said in his heavy French accent, "we make agreement when we invest to give us exclusive rights in all Europe for charging stations. We have not seen zee document to sign."

It was no accident LeBeau bumped into Mack.

Mack looked past LeBeau to see Donovan pacing in the hall. He grinned thankfully at the Frenchman. "Let's go talk with Steve Gray."

By the time they reached the conference table, Gray had rifled through the stack of documents and was holding one up in anticipation.

"Your company's exclusive right to the charging stations for the entire European Union as defined in the investment agreement."

By anticipating LeBeau concern, Gray caught him off guard. "Thank you," was all the Frenchman said. He took the document from Gray and began paging through it.

Mack decided to use LeBeau's review of the agreement as an excuse not to leave. He turned to go tell Donovan only to find Gregorz Pogladek blocking his way.

"What is it Gregorz?" Mack's sharp tone revealed his increasing level of exasperation. "I don't have the time to discuss your new demands."

"I have only one question," Pogladek said raising his finger to indicate the importance of his question. "It is true you loaned a million dollars to Paddy O'May a month ago and as collateral, received the patents and the schematics?"

"Yes and no. My firm, not me, loaned *two* million

dollars to The Celtic Horse to bridge the company until this investment closes. The key word is *loaned*. At the closing, our two million converts to equity and all collateral is released. That happens today." Mack took a step then stopped. "This isn't your first deal, Gregorz. Bridge financing typically happens in deals like this. You know that."

"Now that we know collateral can be pledged, that changes the deal," Pogladek said. "We expect copies of the schematics before we transfer our money." Pogladek thought he had the upper hand.

Mack kept his cool. "You've seen the prototype and drove the car to test the engine. When you stepped out of the vehicle a nuclear holocaust raining down on the world couldn't have wiped the smile off your face. You wanted to invest right then and there."

Pogladek shrugged. "Some of my investors are nervous."

"Get new investors or go find another deal where equity investors get collateral."

Pogladek opened his mouth to reply but no words came out.

Mack stayed silent. He knew no matter what he said,

he'd be negotiating against himself. He waited with a satisfied look on his face, his poker face.

Pogladek wagged his finger and the said, "We are not authorizing our wire transfer until we have a sit down with O'May, Malloy and Sweeney and iron this out. This is their company and they make the final decisions, not you. Or, am I wrong?"

Mack's poker face disappeared. He hadn't anticipated this demand. With O'May missing he had to think fast and come up with a stall tactic that gave him time to find O'May.

"Why Sweeney?" he asked buying time. "He's not an owner."

"He's the Chief Financial Officer. I assume O'May and Malloy rely on his advice and counsel."

Mack wondered why Pogladek made his unreasonable demand *after* he signed the agreement. All investors reviewed the schematics, the drawings and watched numerous test runs. Every single investor was beyond ecstatic with the results they saw. What the investors didn't know was O'May left out a couple details critical to the engine's performance and the recharging process. That was by design. If the designs and schematics the investors had reviewed fell into the wrong hands, hands that tried to replicate the technology, the engine would have trouble powering a two-stroke riding lawn mower. The critical details of the technology were in two places, O'May's head and in a safe deposit box under Mack's name. Only Mack and O'May knew about the safe deposit box.

"You're right, it's the company's decision. Let me talk to them and I'll get back to you."

Pogladek held up his left arm, twisted his wrist to show Mack his watch and said, "Tick, tock."

The phone in Mack's pocket vibrated then rang. He didn't recognize the ring tone and slowly pulled the phone out and realized he still had O'May's phone. He tapped the green icon and brought the phone to his ear praying it was Paddy calling.

"Billy Mack speaking," he answered as he walked away from Pogladek. He looked back to make sure he had walked a safe distance away.

"Good," the voice on the other end of the call said as if he were surprised. After a pause, he said, "*You* are the man I want to speak with. Follow instructions and you may see your little friend again."

"Who is this?" Mack demanded. He tried to place the man's accent. Was it Irish, British or Scottish? Was it someone trying to mock an accent?

"Shut up. I talk, you listen. You will immediately arrange for your bank to wire ten million dollars to an account in Cyprus. After I hang up, you will receive the necessary information in separate text from a different phone. Once you arrange the wire transfer, you go to The Celtic Horse office and wait for instructions. You have thirty minutes to get this done and get to the office. You involve the police and your little friend is dead. By the time you get to the office, we expect to have confirmation of the wire transfer. Once that happens, you will gather up the drawings and schematics and receive further instructions. You don't follow the instructions to the letter, your little friend... dead."

Mack's realized his grip had tightened around the phone and his face burned hot. He exhaled to relax. It didn't work.

"Do you understand, Billy Mack?"

Mack exhaled again. "I need proof Paddy is still alive. I need it before I agree to anything."

"Arrange for the transfer and get to the office in thirty minutes."

"You know it's impossible to arrange a wire transfer in that amount of money in thirty minutes. Hell, the Central Bank of Ireland takes a day just to approve the amount."

"Use your fucking connections."

The phone line went dead.

Mack looked around the room trying to hide his reaction.

He needed Ray Gunn's expertise and experience.

§

CHAPTER 8

Mack replayed the phone call in his head. Something wasn't right. Why was he ordered to initiate a wire transfer that will certainly raise suspicions with the Irish government? And then go to The Celtic Horse office and wait for instructions? Also, why a wire transfer and not cash? Wire transfers are traceable and, more importantly, can be reversed. Either the kidnapper knew something he didn't or he'd seen one too many super-villain movies? He'd run these questions past Ray Gunn.

Before Mack contacted Gunn, he wanted to bounce something off Malloy. He found Malloy standing near Steve Gray, grabbed him by the elbow and led him away from the conference table. Certain sure he was out of earshot of everyone, he stopped and squeezed Malloy's elbow to get him to stop.

"Let me give you a hypothetical," Mack said as preparation for his questions. "Say somebody abducted Paddy, hypothetically, can you think of any reason why?"

Malloy looked at Mack like he was crazy. When Mack's expression didn't change, a wave of panic washed over Malloy. "What reasons-" Malloy stopped in mid-sentence. "Have you heard something?" he said quickly.

Mack knew he couldn't tell Malloy about the phone call and replied, "No, and I've probably seen too many cop shows but it's better to cover all bases."

Malloy began blinking repeatedly as if his brainwaves were misfiring.

"Dig deep, Pius. Can you think of anyone who threatened Paddy or anything that happened to him that doesn't feel right to you?"

Malloy stopped blinking and stood straighter. "Nothing out of the usual. Over the last week or two we had the normal calls from investors, which we directed to you. Paddy only left his workshop to either go home to sleep or to his sister's house to have dinner with her and her husband, Finn. Ever since Paddy and Pius agreed to the investment, Finn would regularly come by the workshop and pick him up. The three of them would have dinner then his sister would drive him home."

"That's it? Think, did anything suspicious happen?"

Malloy raised his eyebrows. "Wait... I overhead him take a call after business hours about a week ago and I could tell from his voice he was agitated. After he hung up, he left and didn't return until the next morning. I asked him about it and he waved me off as if it was nothing, saying it was a personal matter. We didn't discuss again and he's been his normal, eccentric self since."

"Do me a favor, Pius. Go out and keep Paddy's sister busy. Tell her I've been called away to deal with a wire transfer glitch and will be back as soon as I straighten it out and Paddy can get his money. You say that and she'll be fine, I guarantee it."

Clearly unhappy with Mack's request, Malloy closed his eyes and let out a deep breath. A few seconds passed before he slowly opened his eyes and said, "Fine, but you owe me one."

"On second thought," Mack said, "You stay here and mingle. I'll handle the sister."

Malloy grinned like he'd dodged a bullet. "You should know a few things about her. She basically raised Paddy after their father was murdered and their mother drank herself to death. Claire's more of an over-bearing mother than over-bearing sister. She never asks for anything... she demands everything. She's relentless when she wants something and will wear you down. Her husband, Finn is the same way but more subtle."

For as long as he'd known O'May, Mack realized this was the first time anyone spoke of his parents. Mack assumed they were among the living.

"Paddy's father was murdered?" he asked.

Malloy bobbed his head up and down. "Paddy's father, Liam, was IRA (*Irish Republican Army*). Liam was orphaned at a young age and fell in with the Dublin Brigade. He started out in the IRA's robberies group becoming an effective fundraiser and he shot up the ranks. To make a very long story short, Liam, one of, if not *thee* brightest men in the IRA, graduated to bomb making and when Paddy was eleven, his father planted a bomb in Belfast along the route the Ulster Loyalists were planning to march. The bomb was just outside the Catholic neighborhood where the Loyalists were marching through. It was set to detonate as the leaders passed by. A couple hours before the march, a high-ranking Loyalist was out walking with his two sons. The youngest son, who was three, ran into the building where the bomb was planted. The young boy must have jostled the bomb, nobody knows for certain, and the bomb exploded. The Loyalist suspected Liam.

"Six months later, Liam was in Belfast to participate in an IRA march through the Protestant neighborhood and brought Paddy with him, against his mother's wishes. As they were preparing to march, a Loyalist foot soldier, made his was into the middle of the crowd and attacked Liam, stabbing him over twenty times." Malloy paused and took in a breath. "Paddy was a foot or so away and watched the whole ordeal. As you can imagine, panic ensued and Paddy was left there alone, surrounded by a throng of people, all looking down at him and his father."

When Malloy finished, he looked as if he were about to cry. He wiped his eyes.

"That explains a lot," Mack said.

"It's best not to bring it up with Paddy... or even his sister."

"This should be fun," Mack replied as he walked away.

As he approached the conference room door, Mack eyed Claire Donovan out in the hall pacing back and forth along the wall with her cellphone stuck to her ear.

Mack cleared his throat as he entered the hall.

Donovan held up her free hand signaling for Mack to wait until she finished her call.

When Donovan looked at Mack, he held up his wrist and pointed to his watch. He said, "You have ten seconds before I leave."

Donovan ended her call and dropped her phone into her bag.

She glared at Mack expecting an apology. Mack stood silently, not taking his eyes off her.

Thirty seconds later, he said, "Looks like we have a Mexican standoff."

Donovan looked confused. "What?"

"You're the one who demanded I take you to see your brother. What's so urgent?"

Donovan pulled a cigarette case from her bag, put a cigarette between her lips then fumbled through her bag in search of a lighter. She pulled out a gold lighter and lit the end of her cigarette. She sucked in, then let out a long lingering plume of smoke.

"I came here to see if my brother needed my advice and then to help him celebrate. My husband is on his way to join the celebration so I don't need one of his minions giving me the run around." She looked at Mack with a mixture of arrogance and disdain.

Mack was about to pounce on her patronizing arrogance then thought better of it. He had bigger things to worry about. His concern, his focus needed to be on Paddy.

He counted to ten, decompressed and said, "You know Paddy can't be around crowds. We planned for that and prepped him to spend time at the closing dinner, as little time as needed. It's better that way and you know it. If he's forced him to do things he can't or he won't then this deal is as good as dead."

"Fine, fine, my brother is a strange little man. Go find him and bring him to me or take me to him. He needs me."

For some reason, Mack felt like he'd just won a small victory. "Stay here, and I'll go get Paddy." He smiled, politely but firmly.

Mack left her standing with her arms crossed glaring at him like a schoolteacher about to order the class smartass to the principal's office. Mack turned to go find Ray Gunn.

He walked away thinking of who would abduct O'May and why. At the top of the stairs, he paused to think. He understood the $10 million ransom demand: Money. But why ask for the engineering drawings, the schematics?

He thought back on how O'May, Malloy and he worked to get O'May's invention, The Celtic Horse to this point. He recounted everyone they encountered along the way. Maybe that would tell him who abducted Paddy and give him a clue as to his whereabouts.

Prior to forming Celtic Horse, Paddy O'May and Pius Malloy were unemployed, on the dole, they liked to joke, tinkering in O'May's garage with a concept that seemed unrealistic.

Shortly after the two Irishmen became partners, O'May developed a technology that experts were one hundred percent certain defied conventional thinking and the current laws of physics. They believed O'May's idea was a fool's pipe dream. One so-called expert even had the audacity to ask O'May if he could spare some of the opium he was smoking.

In their search for money to finance the concept and bring it to market, Paddy and Pius spent years going hat in hand to anyone with a spare penny — family, friends, banks, angel investors, venture capitalists, loan sharks, you name it. They were repeatedly told the concept was impossible, ill conceived or, if they were being nice, a pipe dream. Most couched their insults as free advice. The first person to believe in their revolutionary concept was Billy Mack and it was about to payoff — big time.

Once Mack invested seed money, Malloy focused on the business side while O'May perfected the prototype. He quickly developed the concept into an electromagnetic engine that managed to go a thousand miles on a single charge. His last iteration improved the technology for the engine to go fifteen hundred miles. O'May wasn't done. His brain wouldn't let him stop.

He'd also designed the recharging mechanisms so that it only took ten minutes to fully recharge and go another fifteen hundred miles. That's equivalent to driving from Chicago to Miami on one tank of gas.

This new-fangled engine defied the laws of physics: For every action there is an equal and opposite reaction. O'May, on the other hand, proved that for every action there is also an even more powerful identical action. The design of the engine and the strong, controlled electrical impulses proved this.

Mack's thoughts came back to The Celtic Horse, an

electromagnetic engine. Such an invention would eliminate the internal combustion engine, upsetting the balance of power and dramatically changing the world as we know it. Powerful people and governments with wealth and power tied up in oil wouldn't know what hit them when the new engine drove onto the market.

The engine had been a very well kept secret until they began their fund raising campaign. All potential investors signed non-disclosure agreements with severe financial penalties if violated. Mack realized that was a moot point, however. Everyone who signed the non-disclosure agreement is a current investor. Spilling the secret would only hurt them and possibly make their investment worth much less. They had too much to lose. Or, did that matter?

Mack was stymied. He came up with only one realistic possibility for why someone abducted O'May: That person had learned about the new engine from an investor and would go to any length to destroy it... and Paddy O'May.

One thing nagged at him. If that was the case and they never wanted the engine to see the light of day, then why are they demanding a $10 million ransom? They could simply kill Paddy. Even if that didn't kill the engine, killing Paddy would delay it hitting the market for years.

Mack shook his head to clear his mind. He fished his phone from his coat pocket and called Ray Gunn.

The call didn't go through. Had Gunn turned off his phone?

§

CHAPTER 9

Mack felt Clair Donovan's eyes burning a hole in his back as he stood at the top of the stairs. He put his phone back into his pocket, turned to go then glanced back at her. She was tapping her foot to send Mack a message - I'm a busy woman and I don't have all day.

Her only redeeming value is that she's not *my* sister, Mack thought with a mental smirk. He quickly realized she could cause a problem with the investors and marched back over to her.

"Paddy won't be coming back until the closing dinner this evening, if he comes to that at all. You know your brother so that should not come as a surprise to you."

"Tell me where he is so I can go to him."

"He didn't tell me where he went."

"I'll call him."

Mack turned and hurried to the stairwell. On the way, he pulled O'May's phone from his pocket and turned off the ringer. As soon as he put the phone on silent, it began to vibrate.

He descended the stairs alternating with two quick steps, two slow steps. The halting rhythm helped him think. A thought came to him. If the kidnappers were after money, there is no way they would have demanded he be at O'May's workshop in thirty minutes.

The ransom demand had to be a diversion, a smoke screen. No investor in The Celtic Horse needed any more money. For all of them, ten million dollars was a drop in the bucket, a weekend in Vegas.

"Keep thinking, Mack," he muttered. He began to worry O'May was expendable and might already be dead. He tried to shake away that thought.

He pushed through the side door of the office building and walked around the corner to the front of the building. He peered around for a taxi. The low, dark gray clouds cast a gloom over everything below it, parroting Mack's emotional state.

A white police car with a thick yellow neon stripe running along the side was parked in front of the main entrance. Fifty feet away, a cop stood outside the main door to the building.

He waved at someone, glanced left and right then stepped inside. Mack wondered if it was standard procedure for Irish cops to work alone?

After the cop disappeared inside, Mack looked up the street in search of a taxi. To his left, he heard the rumble of tires rolling on asphalt. He turned his head to find a line of white police cars speeding toward him. Their lights were on but not their sirens.

The lead car stopped with a subdued screech in front of Mack. The driver stepped out, pointed at Mack and gestured for him not to move. Her chin was barely above the car's roof. She pushed back her thick, red hair and positioned her cap then pulled down on the visor. "Stay where you are, sir," she ordered.

Mack obeyed her order and gave her a reassuring nod.

She marched around the front of the car and stepped up on the curve in front of Mack. She stood a foot shorter than him but gave off an eye-to-eye vibe.

She stepped closer and said, "I'm Detective Bridget Dillon, Criminal Investigation Bureau of Special Crimes Operations. With whom am I speaking?"

"Billy Mack."

Before she could say something, Mack added, "My name is William McMillan, but everyone calls me Billy or Mack."

"Mr. McMillan it is then. What are you doing here?"

Mack thought of about his answer. He knew she was here because of O'May's disappearance. Should he tell her about the ransom demand? If he did, she would never let him leave. Don't lie to the police but don't volunteer information until it's necessary. "I'm trying to hail a taxi to go to the bank."

Dillon quickly asked, "Where are you coming from?"

Mack hesitated again.

Dillon didn't wait. She said, "Blood was found in a men's room in one of the upper floors and there is a reported disappearance that is believed to be connected. Do you know anything about that?"

"Yes," Mack answered, nodding. "I'm going to look for the missing person, Paddy O'May." Mack caught himself and added, "After I go to the bank."

"Do you know the whereabouts of this person?" Dillon's look told Mack she was a human lie detector.

"No, I'm heading to the bank to take care of some urgent business then on to check Paddy O'May's office."

Dillon studied Mack, shifting her lips left and right as she thought. She finally said, "Normally, I wouldn't let you go but when someone disappears time is of the essence."

Relief washed over him. "Thank you."

"Not so fast," she added. "One of my officers will accompany you."

Before Mack could object, she whistled and pointed at an officer with short, black curly hair. The officer was short and lean. Mack noticed his biceps stretched the fabric of his blue uniform shirt and his hands were slightly larger than normal.

"Timmy, I want you to drive Mr. McMillan to his bank then on to the missing person's office," Dillon said.

She turned to Mack and with a foreboding look said, "It'll make me feel better knowing you're safe."

The sarcasm in her voice told Mack to play nice.

"Thank you Detective," he answered.

Officer McNee gestured for Mack to sit in the passenger seat then he looked over at Dillon and asked, "After that Detective, what do you want me to do?"

"Bring him back to me. I'll radio you my location if I'm not here."

Mack pulled the cruiser's door closed and looked over at the cop. He offered the cop his hand. "Billy Mack."

The cop gripped Mack's hand and squeezed. "Timmy McNee, and let's keep the pleasantries to a minimum." His tone was composed, crisp, and military, like his demeanor — all business. His self-assured tone gave Mack a boost of confidence.

"What bank?" he asked.

The drive to the bank took three right hand turns and three minutes. McNee pulled up in front of the bank, put the cruiser in park and stepped out.

Mack remained in the car until McNee stood outside his door.

McNee leaned down and pulled open the door. "Shall we?" he said as if in a hurry.

Mack climbed out. "Thank you officer, but there is no need to go in with me. The business I have to discuss won't take long and is with my personal banker."

"I thought you rich Americans only had Swiss bank accounts?" McNee posed it as a question but Mack knew he meant it as a dig.

"I do have a numbered account in Switzerland," Mack replied and watched to see McNee's reaction.

Officer McNee's face remained stoic.

Mack felt it necessary to explain the account in Dublin and said, "The account here in Dublin is for a company I am investing in here in Ireland."

McNee's expression didn't change. He simply said, "I will go in with you and remain in the bank's lobby. Now let's go." The terms were not up for negotiation.

Mack strolled up to the bank entrance with McNee one-step behind him and to his right.

Inside the bank, McNee stood off to the right and waved for Mack to go transact his business.

Mack walked over to a group of desks on the left

side of the lobby. The desks were aligned three across and four deep. He spoke in a hushed tone to a young brunette sitting at the middle desk in the front row. She nodded as Mack spoke. When he finished, she picked up her phone, punched a number and spoke quietly. She hung up and pointed to a door off to her left then returned to her computer.

Mack glanced back at McNee, caught his attention and mouthed, "Only be a minute."

McNee shrugged as if he didn't care.

Mack knocked and opened the door. He stood in the doorway waiting for the man behind a big desk to look up and wave him in. He stepped inside and closed the door behind him.

"What can I do for you, Mr. McMillan?"

§

CHAPTER 10

The banker's office had light green walls with a row of old black and white photographs of Dublin city-scenes lining all four walls. Mack recognized some of the locations as he strolled up and stood in front of a wooden desk with a green banker's lamp in the corner and large green blotter in the center. The banker, dressed in a blue pinstripe suit, light blue shirt and dark blue tie sat with his hands pressed together as if in prayer. A manila folder sat open in front of him.

"Mr. McMillan, how are you." The banker held his finger up. "When a client shows up without an appointment, that usually means they are not happy with the discharge of my duties. I assure you, we have acted in accordance with your wishes and have done so to the letter." He smiled confidently at Mack.

As the banker spoke, it came back to Mack how prim and proper Rick Ryan struck him. Having worked with a multitude of bankers over the past few years, Mack considered Ryan a banker's banker. He never took off his suit coat, even sitting at his desk.

Mack placed his hands on the desk and leaned slightly forward. "Mr. Ryan, I have no complaints about my account. I am in a hurry so I will dispense with the niceties."

Mack stood up and folded his arms across his chest. "I need ten million dollars wired to an account and I need it done this afternoon, dollars, not Euros."

Ryan sat back and looked at Mack with confusion and defiance.

"That's not possible."

Mack decided he had to go personal. "Rick, You're my banker because you are the best banker in Ireland. You were highly recommended and rightfully so. We have a great working relationship and I plan on expanding it. But, in this case, I'm not asking. I need the money in two hours."

"Billy, I don't know if there is ten million in U.S. dollars available in Ireland. I need to go through the Bank of Ireland. You know that," Ryan replied, keeping it at a personal level.

"You and I both know there is. If you have to pay an above-market exchange rate to get it, keep it reasonable."

"You're asking me to do that before the market closes in two hours. I can't guarantee it can be done."

Mack grinned and said, "When Ray Gunn recommended you he said you could accomplish anything."

When he heard Ray Gunn's name, Ryan steeled himself and stood. He said, "It will get done."

Mack heard the door behind him open. He twisted around to see McNee standing in the doorway, expressionless.

Mack closed his eyes and pursed his lips. He didn't want his banker to see that he came to the bank with a police escort.

"I'm almost done here Timmy and will be right out."

"That's fine, I'll wait with the door open." McNee took a step back.

Mack read suspicion on Ryan's face and didn't like the look. Before Ryan could ask a question, Mack said, "If you have any questions, call Ray Gunn."

This time Ryan cringed when he heard Ray Gunn's name and fell back into his chair.

The banker looked over at McNee standing just outside the door. "If you give me the wire transfer instructions, I will complete the transaction as requested and in the time needed."

Mack stuck his hand out, reaching across the desk. "I'll text you the account information once I've confirmed it. Thank you, Rick." He had the account information on O'May's phone but knew once the transfer was complete he and O'May were both dead.

He tried to read the banker's face.

Ryan's eyes were stuck on the cop but his mind was elsewhere.

Mack turned and marched out of the office. He took a glance back to see Ryan lifting his phone to his ear. Mack hoped he was calling Ray Gunn.

Inside the police cruiser, Mack kept his eyes forward as they pulled into the street.

"You want to tell me what business you had to transact at the bank?" McNee asked. It was more an order than a question.

"No." Now it was Mack's turn to be a man of few words.

They drove in silence for a couple minutes. Mack could feel McNee getting antsy, dying to say something.

Mack sat stone-faced as he watched the buildings pass by. Out of the corner of his eye he detected McNee gripping the steering wheel so tight his fingers turned red.

McNee couldn't take it any longer. "You do know when we return to Detective Dillon you will have to tell her the reason for the visit to the bank." He relaxed his grip on the steering wheel.

"Yes, I know." Mack knew if he told McNee about the ransom demand, the police would immediately take over, meaning Paddy was good as dead. O'May was already on thin ice. If Mack showed up with a cop in tow — explicitly against the orders of the kidnappers — Paddy's life was over.

"Take the next left then the second right," Mack said. "In the middle of that block, let me out and I will walk the half block to the building on the right corner, on the opposite side of the cross street."

"My orders are to accompany you. I already bent the

rules once at the bank."

A half block from O'May's workshop, Mack pointed to the right and said, "Pull over right here." Mack could see a cop's trained suspicion all over McNee's face. He had to come up with something plausible to keep McNee in the car.

"Look, Paddy O'May is very eccentric and I need to prepare him that a stranger will be coming, give him time to reduce his anxiety."

McNee shot Mack a do-you-think-I'm-stupid look. "It doesn't take a rocket scientist to figure out what's going on. Mr. O'May has been abducted. The stop at the bank was to arrange the ransom and now you're meeting the kidnappers to tell them you've arranged for the payment and will have it for them this afternoon."

Mack remembered his rule not to lie to a cop. He sat silently, his gaze fixed on the building up ahead. The two story, red brick workshop was in desperate need of repairs.

McNee placed his hand on Mack's shoulder. He had a somber look on his face, as if he knew what was in store for Mack. "In these situations, odds are, your friend is already dead. If not, he will be as soon as you pay the ransom. There's also a better than even chance you will be killed as soon as you deliver the ransom."

Mack couldn't bring himself to look at McNee. "I don't have a choice."

McNee pulled his pistol from his side holster and held it in front of Mack. He studied the building and said, "Maybe we do."

§

CHAPTER 11

McNee explained his plan to Mack. When he finished he had a pugnacious grin on his face. He looked excited, almost giddy at the anticipation of action.

Mack somberly nodded his agreement.

McNee stepped out the cruiser. He turned and put one hand on the door the other on the roof of the car. He leaned down and stuck his head back inside.

"Remember, give me five minutes to get inside then approach the building. Walk up nervously. That's what they expect." McNee closed the door and walked from the cruiser, heading away from the workshop.

Billy looked down at his watch. Walk nervously, he thought. That won't be hard to do.

When the time came, he stepped out, surveyed the street and took a step. He felt a tinge of apprehension, not for his safety but the ugly anticipation of finding Paddy O'May's dead body. He shook the negativity from his mind and headed toward the workshop.

Mack walked nervously. It wasn't an act. He thought about O'May. A brilliant mind but more importantly, a good guy, someone Mack was fortunate, even honored to know.

At the main door, Mack knocked twice and stepped back and to the side. Thirty seconds later, he stepped up and knocked again, this time harder, pounding on the door.

He waited a few seconds then turned the door handle. It was unlocked. He opened the door a few inches and waited. He heard the rev of an engine down the street. He turned to see a car racing toward him. The car slowed as it approached the workshop. The driver looked at Mack, grinned then hit the gas and raced away.

Mack waited until the car drove out of sight then pushed open the door. Inside, he stood silently, his senses on high alert.

He headed toward the office, his steps deliberate as he listened for any noise. The narrow hallway heightened

Mack's uneasiness.

The office door was wide open. The office seemed smaller than he remembered. Inside were two small desks pushed together and two metal filing cabinets against the far wall. There wasn't room for anything else.

Mack made his way down the hall to the workshop. He pushed open the metal door and stood back. He heard someone moving around inside.

He leaned his head into the doorway and yelled, "This is Billy Mack and I'm coming in."

After a short pause, he heard, "I cleared the place. Come on in." It was McNee's voice.

Then McNee yelled, "Somebody was here earlier judging by the coffee cups on the table."

Mack walked into the room, saw O'May's coffee cup and said, "That's Paddy's coffee cup so it had to be from earlier in the day."

Mack walked over to McNee who stood next to the Celtic Horse studying the engine, in a vehicle that looked like it came from a Sci-Fi movie.

The workshop was the size of a mechanic's garage. There were two large garage doors, a grease pit on the left side where mechanics stood beneath the car to work on the undercarriage. The Celtic Horse would never be in need of a grease pit.

On the right side, the body of a silver Mercedes Benz sedan rested atop a large steel contraption. The four tires were resting on two thick hard rubber rollers, in the front and back of each tire. The hood over the engine was missing and a number of thick wires and tubes ran from the engine to a bank of computers standing on a long table against the wall.

McNee leaned over and stared down at the engine. "What the hell is this?" he asked without looking up.

"It's an invention O'May is working on."

McNee, still staring at the engine, said, "I've never seen anything like this. What the hell is it?" McNee looked over to Mack. "Are those magnets?"

Mack strolled over to the car. "That's a modified electromagnetic engine, Paddy O'May's version."

"How does it work?"

"Only O'May can explain exactly how but it has to do with how electric pulses drive the magnets which act like pistons."

McNee shook his head. "How the hell did he figure that out?"

"He thinks differently than everyone else."

"That's an understatement."

McNee stepped back and scanned the workshop. "I thought you said the kidnappers were meeting you here?"

Mack shrugged. "Those were my instructions."

McNee pointed straight up. "What's upstairs?"

"I don't know. Somebody else rents that space."

"I'm going to do one more sweep, see if I missed something. You stay here."

McNee marched away and back toward the office. Two minutes later he strolled back in. "It seems your kidnappers are a no show."

Mack glanced down at his watch. "Let's give them ten more minutes." He thought for a second and added, "It may make sense if you're out of sight when they arrive. They were very explicit about me not going to the cops."

McNee scratched his head as he thought about giving the kidnappers more time and whether he should stay with Mack.

"If they show up, they are not going to have O'May with them... unless they're really stupid."

"I don't know what to tell you."

McNee grimaced as if he didn't want to say what he was about to say.

"Fine, I'll stay out of sight but within earshot, just in case." He turned and headed back toward the office.

Mack stood by the car and examined the engine while he waited. He knew that once the engine hit the market, competitors would try to reverse engineer the technology. That wouldn't be too difficult. He knew however, the technology of the charging station would be near impossible to duplicate and the secret to it was only in O'May's head. If someone were able reverse engineer the charging technology, it would take years to develop it.

Ten minutes later, McNee came back into the workshop. "Your kidnappers are a no show. I'm bringing you back to Detective Dillon."

Mack started to argue then thought better of it. He had O'May's phone in his pocket and whoever abducted

O'May could contact him.

They walked slowly back to the front door. As Mack reached for the handle, McNee said, "I'll ask Dillon to be assigned to you until we get your friend back, if we get your friend back."

Mack pushed open the door. Two men dressed in black stood a couple feet away with pistols aimed at them.

The taller man on the left, fired twice, hitting McNee in the chest. He fell back, his head bouncing off the hard concrete.

McNee lay on the ground, his arms and legs sprayed wide as if he stopped in the middle of making a snow angel.

Before Mack could react, the man on the right jammed his pistol under Mack's chin.

"I said no cops." He pushed his pistol up forcing Mack to raise his chin. "You even breath and that's the last thing you'll ever do."

The taller man who shot McNee grabbed Mack by the nape of his neck and pushed him toward a white workman's van parked partially up on the sidewalk. He shoved Mack inside and jumped in behind him. The other kidnapper pulled the side door closed, slamming hit hard.

Inside, the kidnapper wrestled a hood over Mack's head and pushed him down onto his side. He kicked Mack in the ribs and said, "What part of no cops didn't you understand?"

He felt a rib crack on his left side. The air in his lungs rushed out and he gasped to get air back into his lungs. He braced for another kick but it never came.

"Keep your mouth shut until I tell you to talk," the kidnapper screamed in Mack's ear.

Mack's hands were slapped together and a thick rope was wrapped tightly around his wrists.

The engine started up and the van squealed away.

As soon as Mack's breathing returned he had only one thought. He'd seen the kidnappers faces.

That was a death sentence.

§

CHAPTER 12

Mack concentrated on the clock in his head, timing the trip in seconds. The van moved swiftly, accelerating rapidly and powering through turns. He kept track of the turns, left, right, left, right. It seemed they were driving in circles, clearly to avoid a tail. He listened for the kidnappers to say something. They never did.

Seven minutes later, a rough guess by Mack, the van slowed to stop. He heard a metal rolling on metal. He guessed it was a large garage door rolling open. A few seconds later, the rolling stopped. The only the sound was that of the idling engine. The van inched forward and rolled to a stop.

The van door slid open and someone grabbed him by the ankle and pulled him out. He landed hard on his butt. A shock of pain from his cracked rib reverberated through his body. He stifled a moan.

Two men grabbed him by the biceps and pulled him forward. Mack stumbled and the men let him fall. By reflex, he twisted as he fell to land on his right shoulder. It didn't make a difference. A sharp pain from his cracked rib shot through him. He grunted as he rolled onto his back.

The two men laughed as they yanked him up.

"Don't worry, once we get our money you won't be in pain anymore."

Both men laughed hysterically as they pulled Mack with them.

A door creaked open. A hand on his back pushed him inside then grabbed the hood and slowly pulled it off.

Mack turned to see the tall kidnapper grinning wildly, directly in contrast to the indifference in his eyes which said life had little value to him.

The kidnapper untied Mack's hands and shoved him further into the room.

"If I hear anything, a cough, a sneeze, I'll break a few more ribs." He spun around, walked out and slammed the door behind him.

The sound of two heavy latches being clamped together echoed through the empty room. Above the door a dim light came on. It shined no stronger than a tiny nightlight but enough for Mack to get his bearings.

After a few seconds, Mack's eyes adjusted. The windowless, dank room stunk of urine and feces. The walls, ceiling and floor were dark. In the corner stood a dirty plastic bucket. Mack assumed it's original color was white.

Mack rubbed his wrists as he approached the bucket. The stink penetrating his nose grew stronger. The empty bucket lay on its side and, as he neared, the smell staggered him.

He quickly moved to the opposite corner and lowered himself down. He gently massaged his sore ribs. It was time to think.

He'd seen the kidnappers faces and knew exactly what that meant. The kidnapper so much as told him. He had one choice. Figure a way out. He studied the room for any cracks or weaknesses. It was too dim to determine any.

He pushed himself up bracing his back against the

wall. He stood and rotated his left shoulder. The pain in his chest stung but was manageable. The rib is only cracked, he thought.

He heard a noise, crept over to the door and pressed his ear against it. A door in the other room opened and closed. The click of heels moved steadily across the room. He heard a woman's muted voice.

"How are our two guests?" she asked.

Mack tried to identify her accent - Irish, Scottish, British?

"Resting comfortably."

Mack recognized the voice of the taller kidnapper who then let out a sly chuckle. "Do you want to check on them?"

"That's a bad idea. I don't want either of them to see my face."

"What does that matter? Once I get my share, they won't be around to tell anyone."

"I'll notify you once the money is in the account. Then get rid of the American. I don't want his body found. I don't care how you do it."

"What about the little muppet?"

After a pause and a clearing of the throat, the woman's voice said, "I need him alive and unharmed for now."

For the next thirty seconds, there was complete silence before the woman's voice returned, this time much louder.

She yelled, "Why are you flustered?" Her tone quieted but remained stern. "I can see it in your face. You had specific orders not to harm him. What the hell did you do to him?"

"He's fine, a little cut and bruised up but fine," the taller kidnapper replied. "He wasn't very cooperative and we did what we needed to do."

"There is more to this deal than you know. Don't touch him again, understand?"

The steady click of heels moved back across the floor. A door opened and closed.

Mack pulled his ear from the door. Why didn't the kidnappers ask about the wire transfer?

Mack circled the room to stretch his legs and loosen up. As he walked along a sidewall, he heard O'May's voice. It was faint but definitely his voice. It bled through the wall. He moved methodically along the wall feeling for anything, a weakness, a soft spot in the wall, anything he could use. His steps were light and rather than pound on the walls he pressed hard, making no noise.

O'May's voice stopped but Mack continued his probing, searching.

After an hour of silence, he gave up and returned to the door. He pressed his back against the door, slid down and sat on the cold floor.

He heard a door in the room next to him open. The voice of the taller kidnapper rang out. "Get up, muppet and there'll be no trouble from you."

"Where am I going?" O'May asked, his voice full of fear.

"Shut the fuck up."

Mack marched over to the door to listen.

Nothing.

Mack slid down the wall and sat.

He awoke from his dozing when he heard

commotion on the other side of the door. He pressed his ear against the door and held his breath so he could hear better.

He heard two quick muffled sounds, like air from a tire but in two bursts.

There were moans and then a loud howl of pain from a male voice. Mack recognized the voice of the taller kidnapper as he begged, "No, please. I'm on your side."

Mack tried to decipher the commotion. Something dragging across the floor then dropped in a thud. The taller kidnapper whined then began crying.

Mack heard footsteps coming toward the door. He winced in pain as he rolled away from the door in order to be hidden behind the opened door. The two latches clicked and the door flung open.

A hand holding a pistol with a suppressor attached emerged from behind the door and froze.

Mack's mind ordered him to rush the door and put his shoulder into it then grab the pistol and get the advantage. He lowered his shoulder and ran at the door.

He hit the door with his left shoulder. A jolting pain shot through his body as the door slammed shut. Mack dropped to his knees and grabbed his ribcage. He was in shock that the door had closed so easily. That wasn't in the plan.

With his free hand, he wiped the sweat from his brow and opened his eyes. His vision was blurry.

As the pain subsided, he used the door as a crutch and pulled himself up.

Five feet to his right stood the hazy outline of a woman holding a pistol in her right hand, pointing it at the ground between them.

Mack squeezed his eyes shut then blinked repeatedly to bring them into focus.

"Billy, are you okay?"

§

CHAPTER 13

It took thirty seconds for Mack's eyes to regain their focus. His right hand unconsciously massaged his rib cage. He tried to suck in a deep breath to relieve the pain but the stench from the dirty bucket reflexively beat that back.

The woman took a step toward Mack. She came into focus.

"Anna Swerdlov?" He said, unable to hide the surprise in his voice. He looked at her, then down at the gun in her right hand before twisting his head to assess the door. As he turned back, he asked, "Where's the big guy who abducted me?"

She grinned and replied, "He's in the other room."

Mack glanced back at the gun and steeled himself. "Do what you're going to do and if you have a shred of decency, do it quick."

Swerdlov stepped close to Mack and said, "That's exactly the reaction I expected from you."

Her face grew rigid as her eyes drilled into his.

Mack stroked his chin with the palm of his hand and waited. He held her gaze as he tried to figure out why she was there.

He finally shook his head and said, "Falcon Investments, I should have known. Your firm has a shady reputation and I argued vehemently against you playing in the deal but Ray Gunn overruled me."

Mack detected a glimmer of empathy in Swerdlov. It vanished as quick as it appeared.

"Let's go get Paddy O'May," she said, her tone all business, like it was her job. "Lead the way." She flicked her pistol toward the door.

Mack didn't move, he simply shrugged and said, "He was in the room next to this one." He pointed to the sidewall. "From the sound of things, I believe someone took him away." Mack walked over to the door.

"Stop," Swerdlov ordered. "Did you just say he's not here?"

Mack shrugged again. "Why are you surprised? Those were your orders."

"What are you talking about?"

Mack read her face. She looked genuinely confused. Mack replayed the conversation he heard when he'd pressed his ear against the door. He was having difficulty recalling the woman's voice.

"An hour or two ago, I heard a conversation between a woman and one of the kidnappers. The voices were faint but I could hear well enough through the door. The woman, who since you are here I assume is you, ordered the kidnapper to kill me once the wire transfer was complete. As soon as the conversation was over-"

Swerdlov cut him off. "Wire transfer? What wire transfer?"

"The ten million dollars I was ordered to transfer to a numbered account in Nico BancPrivat in Nicosia, Cyprus."

"Nico BancPrivat? That's Sunden Capital's main bank."

Mack nodded.

Swerdlov stepped around Mack and pulled the door open. "Whew, I can't take the stink in this room any longer."

Mack followed her out. The thought of rushing her entered his mind.

As if she read his mind, she said, "Don't do anything stupid Billy, my piece has a hair trigger." She turned and gave Mack a look that told him not to move an inch.

"I seem to be missing something," Mack said. "Your reaction tells me you don't know about the ransom."

Swerdlov marched over to the door to the other room and pushed it open.

Mack followed, staying ten feet behind.

The empty room had the same overwhelming stench. Swerdlov slammed the door shut and turned to Mack. "How long ago did they take him away?"

"To the best of my recollection, close to two hours ago."

"Follow me," she said and strolled across the room to a storage closet. She reached down and pulled the tall kidnapper out by the leg. She dropped his leg onto the concrete.

The semiconscious kidnapper moaned weakly. His pants were soaked in blood down to the knee.

Swerdlov kicked him in the ribs.

He grunted and his eyes flickered open.

She bent down and brought her lips to within an inch of his ear. She pressed her pistol hard against the center of his chest.

"When was Paddy O'May taken from here?"

The kidnapper whimpered then said, "I don't know."

Swerdlov stepped over and pushed the barrel of the gun into his groin. "You have a choice. Tell me what I want to know and you can keep your other ball."

"Two hours ago," he said.

"Where was he taken?"

"I don't know."

"Wrong answer."

The kidnapper raised his hands but not his arms. He lifted head a few inches. "I could lie to you and buy time until you came back but I wasn't involved in the planning.

I'm not told shit. I'm paid to do what I'm told. My job is to kill the America and hide his body. For that I get paid handsomely. Go ahead and shoot me... I would."

Mack walked over to Swerdlov. "Ask him about the woman here earlier?"

Swerdlov nudged the kidnapper's leg. "Well, you heard him. Who is she?"

The kidnapper raised his head again. "I wasn't given a name, just a description."

"Who gave you the description?"

"The man who hired me."

Swerdlov stepped in between the man's legs and jammed her right foot into the man's bloody groin. "What's your name?"

"Jennings, Mikey Jennings."

"Who hired you, Mikey Jennings?"

"I never got a name. He was American, a little guy with a bag of money."

"Nobody pays a moron like you in advance," Swerdlov said and pressed down with her right foot.

The kidnapper squirmed and grimaced until she eased the pressure.

"I got a thousand in advance the rest would come after I finish the job."

"When did the meet take place?"

"Last week. A blacked out Range Rover outside Mulligans on Poolbeg Street picked me up and dropped me off at the airport with specific instructions where to find the down payment. After I got my money, I was told to wait for further instructions. The next day someone called me and told me what to do."

"Who called you?"

"A woman with a funny accent. She gave me my marching orders and hung up."

"What else should I know?"

"I had to pay for my own way back to the city."

Swerdlov lifted her foot from his groin, stepped back and chewed on her lip in thought. She pointed to Mack and then to the closet. "Put him back in there."

Mack shook his head. "You can't just let him die."

Swerdlov grinned nonchalantly. "Someone will be

here shortly to pick him up and get him medical attention."

Mack snapped a picture of the kidnappers face with O'May's phone. He grimaced from the pain in his ribs as he dragged the kidnapper back into the closet. The kidnapper moaned then began to sob as Mack stepped over him and closed the door.

Swerdlov had her phone in her ear and gestured for Mack to stay quiet. She hung up and said, "Someone will be here in fifteen."

Mack folded his arms across his chest. "What the hell is going on?"

She ignored his question. "Are you sure it was Nico BancPrivat in Cyprus?"

"Of course, why?"

"That's not important right now." Swerdlov walked away from Mack and stood near the door to the street. She stared off in the distance, thinking.

She turned and asked, "Did you see the other kidnapper?"

"Yes, the smaller one was a few inches shorter than me but bulkier. He looked like he worked out regularly.

He was also missing a front tooth."

"Black hair, short?"

Mack nodded.

"At least something's going my way," she said.

"You want to fill me in?" Mack asked.

Swerdlov raised her finger. "I need to make another call first. Stay here."

She opened the door and stepped out onto the sidewalk.

§

CHAPTER 14

Mack stepped out onto the sidewalk and shivered from the damp cold. The wind had kicked up and the low gray clouds looked like they wanted to spit out rain.

Swerdlov stood out in the street talking quietly on her phone. Mack couldn't hear her and strolled toward her.

Without turning around, Swerdlov swung her left arm behind her with her palm up, ordering Mack to stop.

Frustrated, Mack folded his arms across his chest and pricked up his ears. He only heard, "Thanks Ray, I'll fill Billy in on what he needs to know."

Mack waited for Swerdlov to approach with his back and his expression both rigid. "Why did you tell Ray Gun,

'I'll fill Billy in on what he needs to know?'"

Swerdlov sighed like she didn't want to tell him but had no choice.

"First, let me caveat everything I'm about to tell you with this: You were being used but were never meant to be involved. What I mean-"

Mack's fists balled up tightly, matching his composure.

She realized she was getting nowhere and raised her hands defensively. "To make a long story short, when I infiltrated Falcon Investments, their major investor asked if I could set you up. I agreed. Then-"

"Infiltrated?" Mack asked, cutting her off.

Swerdlov put her hand on Mack's forearm. "Let me finish then I'll answer your questions... the questions I can answer." She waited for Mack to acknowledge her.

Mack shrugged his right shoulder then grimaced from the pain shooting through his left rib cage.

If Swerdlov noticed his reaction, she didn't acknowledge it. "I was working in Moscow when I met J Otis Weil, who I believe you know. For any number of reasons, he despises you, claiming you've fucked him over too many times — his words, not mine. He wanted my help. I needed to be in his good graces and for him to trust me so I agreed to help."

She studied Mack's stone cold face and smiled meekly hoping to take the sting out of her words.

The faint sound of multiple sirens caught Mack's ear. Swerdlov gripped Mack's arm and spun him a half turn.

She said, "Let's finish this in my car."

Her grip was firm and tight. Mack made a halfhearted effort to wriggle free.

She released her grip and said, "The Guards will take Jennings to get medical attention, giving us more time."

In the middle of the next block, Swerdlov lifted a key fob and squeezed it with her thumb. The door locks to a silver Jaguar clicked open. Out of habit, Mack walked to what he thought was the passenger side.

"Other side, Billy."

Inside the car, Mack wasn't about to look at Swerdlov and kept his concentration on the red brick building they'd just left.

Swerdlov said, "Maybe I should turn on the heat to get rid of that cold shoulder of yours."

Mack kept his eyes on the building. "Why were you in Moscow and why did you have to get J Otis to trust you?" Mack asked.

"I can't tell you that. Besides, it's now irrelevant to what's going on with you."

"Why do I feel like I'm still being used?"

"Like I said earlier, Billy, you were not meant to be involved. J Otis Weil wanted you dead... wants you dead. The plan I came up with was... is designed to protect you, keep you safe from J Otis Weil and give me time to do what I have to do."

Mack slowly turned his head and waited for Swerdlov to look at him.

"Did Ray Gunn sign off on your plan?"

"I didn't need his sign off. He was against it, if that makes you feel better. After he realized he had no say, he reviewed my plan. He liked it but acknowledged that every plan goes awry and I needed to be prepared for anything."

"Not a very well thought out plan, if you asked me."

"You were a baseball player once. From what Ray Gunn told me, a very good one at that. Is that correct?"

"I played."

"Apparently, baseball players have to be ready to react to multiple possibilities. When they expect the other team to do something, they set up a defense or a play for that, right?"

"Usually."

"And when the unexpected happens, players know how to react, or am I wrong?"

"So the unexpected happened here?"

"Yes, after the closing dinner, I was to entice you to my hotel where J Otis would have a team ready to snatch you up and spirit you off to Moscow. That was my part in J Otis' plan, to get you to the hotel."

"You seem confident I'd go with you."

"That's what I wanted to talk to you about earlier. You were never meant to go to the hotel. I had a stand-in, a professional who could be your twin brother to act as you. We also had an armed team in position to intervene." Swerdlov lifted her phone. "Ray Gunn made me promise you would not be involved. Call and ask him."

Mack shook his head. "Was Paddy's kidnapping, or

disappearance, part of the plan?"

"As far as I know, J Otis was focused solely on you. However, from what I've learned, he deals with everyone on a need-to-know basis. That makes me assume he's involved in Paddy's disappearance."

Mack found himself nodding in agreement. "J Otis is pure evil and he's smart. You're exactly right, he'll only tell you what he wants you to hear. He fancies himself a master manipulator, a chess player with human pieces. Nothing is out of bounds with him."

"Why would he be involved in O'May's kidnapping?" Swerdlov asked.

Mack took a few seconds to answer. "Falcon Investments is heavily funded by Sunden Capital, J Otis' firm, as well as by a number of Russian Oligarchs, including their President. Once Paddy's engine hits the market, the oil and gas industry will basically dry up. The Russian economy is a one-trick pony and will collapse, making Russia a third world country."

"That doesn't tell me why J Otis is involved... besides his lust to kill you."

"J Otis basically works for the Russian President. He does the man's dirty work. It's a brilliant relationship. If anyone tries to connect the Russian President with a murder, a bribe, any crime you can name, he'll point to the American, J Otis Weil."

"I always knew of their connection but not to the level you're describing'" Swerdlov said.

The sirens grew louder.

"Those sirens bring me back to my earlier statement of a plan not very well thought out."

Swerdlov opened her arms with her palms up.

"As I told you, in my business, things go awry more often than not. If you want out, I'll drive you to where ever you want."

"I want to go rescue Paddy. Whatever it takes."

Swerdlov laughed easily. "Ray Gunn said you always do the right thing."

Mack tapped the steering wheel. "What are we waiting for?"

"Ray Gunn has arranged for Nimesh to call me. He'll handle the technology to help us find O'May."

"You know Nimesh?" Mack asked, surprised to hear his name.

"Everyone in my business knows Nimesh or knows of him. How do you think I found you?"

"Your business?"

Swerdlov grinned widely. "Do I need to spell it out for you?"

"No, but I need to know what to expect."

Up ahead, in front of the brick building, five police cruisers screeched to a halt with sirens screaming and lights flashing. Eight officers flew out onto the street and rushed inside. A short redhead climbed out of lead car and perused the neighborhood, her hands resting on her hips. Detective Dillon looked calm, assured.

Swerdlov handed her phone to Mack. "When Nimesh calls, answer."

She pushed the ignition button and started the car. As she pulled out, Mack saw Dillon turn and blatantly point to the brick building.

Mack detected a sly smile on Swerdlov's face and a slight nod as she did a U-turn.

§

CHAPTER 15

Swerdlov turned at the first right, drove two blocks then pulled the car over in front of a shuttered bookstore. "We wait here for Nimesh's call." She held her hand out for Mack to give her back her phone.

"I think I'll hang on to it for now," he said. He looked at the black screen and saw the reflection of his face. He needed a shave.

"Ray also said you can be stubborn as a mule."

"Sometimes that's a good trait to have and in that vain, I want some answers."

"Like I said, I'll answer the questions I can."

Mack placed his left hand on his sore left rib cage. "I think I'm entitled to the answers I want. Let's start at the beginning." Mack smiled at how that sounded. "Why were you in Russia?"

"You don't need to know."

"Yes I do. It occurred to me that you're after J Otis, and in order for you to bring him down you need me. If I'm out of the picture, you lose your connection to him."

As soon as Swerdlov shifted in her seat, Mack knew he had her and she would answer.

"J Otis, with help from Russian and pro-Russian Ukrainian thugs, runs an international sex trafficking ring of teenage girls in Europe and, to a lesser extent, North America. The ring targets girls between thirteen and fifteen. I'm leading the operation to bring J Otis and the ring down. I will do whatever it takes."

"This sounds personal."

"What J Otis is doing is despicable."

"Agreed, but that doesn't tell me why it's personal."

Mack waited for Swerdlov to collect her thoughts. He wasn't about to rush her.

Swerdlov cleared her throat as if her thoughts were difficult to put into words. Her eyes grew moist and faintly red.

"Two years ago, my little sister Alexa went on a school trip to St. Petersburg. While there, she went to my father's hometown of Virki in Russia to visit my aunt. Virki is a tiny town east of St. Petersburg. Alexa and her cousin took the bus into St. Petersburg to meet up with her classmates, sightsee and shop. That evening, they had a half hour to wait for the bus back to Virki. She and my cousin, along with some schoolmates, went into an ice cream shop. Alexa and one girl went to the bathroom in the back of the shop and never came out. The police found their purses and phones in a dumpster behind the shop."

Swerdlov closed her eyes and inhaled deeply to keep from crying.

"I'm sorry," Mack said softly.

Swerdlov collected herself and continued, "After a week of no clues and no sign of her, the police moved on. My father's best friend growing up took up the case and uncovered information believed to lead to the sex ring. A month into his investigation, the cops found his dead body, shot twice in the face."

"What did he uncover?"

"The area of St. Petersburg where this shop is located has had a number of teenage girls disappear over the last five years. The ice cream shop is closely watched. The owner was using the shop to launder money that is likely tied to the sex trade. He was found dead a week later. I believe the trail leads to the Russian mafia and J Otis Weil."

Swerdlov opened the console, pulled out a picture of her sister and showed Mack. "I took this a few days before she left for Virki."

He fixated on the beautiful young blonde in the picture. "She's beautiful. How old was she when this was taken?"

"I took it just before her fourteenth birthday which she wanted to celebrate with her cousin. They were close."

Mack's eyes followed the picture as Swerdlov gingerly placed it back inside the console.

The phone in Mack's hand vibrated. He recognized Nimesh's number and tapped the screen.

"Put it on speaker," Swerdlov said.

Mack tapped the screen twice and said, "Hi Nims, it's Billy. I'm with Anna Swerdlov."

"Billy? I'm glad Anna got to you in time."

"From what I hear it's thanks to you."

"I only pinged Padraig O'May's phone. Anna had to walk into the lion's den."

"We don't have time to chat," Swerdlov said. "Were you able to ping the other phones from Billy's location?"

"Both phones are burners. One of them is still in Billy's previous location. The other phone is on the move. That's the kidnapper I'm assuming has Padraig O'May. It stopped twice in the last hour for ten minutes each time. I hacked into the closed circuit camera network for Dublin but have been unable to identify the vehicle... yet. O'May could be at either location or still on the move. I've sent the two locations to Anna's phone with GPS instructions for the fastest way there."

"You said the phone is on the move. Where is it headed?" Swerdlov asked.

"It's headed north. If I had to guess, I'd say it's heading to the airport."

"Why would the kidnapper take Paddy to a public place like the airport?"

"You're assuming O'May is still in the vehicle. I'll call you back when the phone, the vehicle stops." Nimesh hung up without waiting for a reply.

Mack brought up the first location on Swerdlov's phone. The GPS clicked on and instructed them to turn left in two hundred yards.

They drove in silence, both lost in their thoughts.

Mack finally broke the silence. "After the murder of your father's friend was anything else done to locate your sister?"

Swerdlov thought about her answer. After the GPS voice instructed her to take the next right, she said, "My parents and the parents of the other girl hired a private investigator in St. Petersburg. They met with him there. He did some digging then quit and tried to talk my parents into letting the police re-work the case. My father followed up with some of the people his childhood friend met and a couple days later, my parents were killed in a car crash... it was not an accident."

"Most likely," Mack said.

"Not most likely, I know for a fact they were murdered because they were investigating the sex ring. I've been working this for two years. That's how I learned of the connection to J Otis Weil."

"How were you able to confirm that information when your father and his friend were unable?"

"I used the information from them and put one and one together. I identified the man who tipped off J Otis and his thugs of each investigation. He was well paid."

"How do you know this guy didn't give you up to J Otis?"

"Because I was the last person he ever talked to."

Mack slowly turned his head, about to ask her how she knew that.

She quickly added, "Let's leave it at that."

The phone in Mack's hand vibrated again. Nimesh was calling back.

Mack put the phone on speaker, held it up and said, "Hi Nims, what do you have for us?"

There was pause then Nimesh said, "This is bad news."

"Is it Paddy?" Mack asked.

After another pause Nimesh answered, "Nothing new on Paddy. The vehicle has stopped at the FBO terminals at Dublin Airport."

"Where the private jets are based?"

"What's the bad news, Nimesh?" Swerdlov asked.

"I think the infamous Becca just arrived in Dublin. Earlier today, a private jet belonging to the FSB left Moscow. An hour into the flight, the pilot radioed a change of destination - Dublin. The plane is carrying five passengers, a man and four women. The man is a diplomatic officer at the Russian Embassy in Dublin. That means he's FSB and is giving the others diplomatic cover."

"How do you know that?" Mack asked.

"Diplomatic officers at embassies are always spies and when they travel, don't go through a normal customs check, just passport verification."

"That means we have no way of knowing what weapons were brought in." Swerdlov said.

"What about the other passengers?" Mack asked.

"The names are aliases but the customs officer described them in detail: two beautiful young women, teenagers made up to look like adults and a slender blonde wearing all black. The blonde was stern, distant, and all business. All she told customs was she 'is in Dublin on business.'" Nimesh sighed and added, "They exited the FPO and were picked up by a black Range

Rover. The airport security cameras picked up the car and sitting in the back seat was a small, wiry man with bad hair plugs. That definitely describes J Otis Weil and he's brought in the best."

"I'm shocked he sent for her," Swerdlov said, barely above a whisper.

"Her? This... Becca?" Mack asked.

§

CHAPTER 16

Swerdlov snatched the phone out of Mack's hand and clicked it into a cradle attached to the dashboard. A street map of Dublin appeared on the screen.

"Who is Becca and why is FSB involved?" Mack asked.

Swerdlov stroked her left cheek then said, "Becca is an assassin, the best in the world. The FSB is the Russian State Security Service, basically the successor to the KGB and work directly for the Russian President."

"Who determines the best assassin in the world?" Mack asked, almost smiling at the ranking.

"The CIA, NSA, MI5, MI6, Mossad, to name few. Do I need to go on? She gets at least a million dollars for a successful job... up front. She's never had to give back any money."

Mack let the million-dollar fee sink in.

"You're telling me she's in Dublin to kill me?"

"Either you or Paddy... or more likely both."

Mack stiffened. "If Paddy is a target and is in that car at the airport, he's already dead."

"I don't think so. Becca is extremely cautious. There are too many cameras around and people who may be looking out their office windows. She doesn't leave witnesses. The more likely scenario is she instructs the kidnapper to drive her and the target out to a secluded spot in the country. She kills them both then sets fire to the vehicle."

"You sound like you admire her."

"Far from it, I respect and fear her skills. I'd be a fool not to."

"Fear? That doesn't instill any confidence in me."

"Fear is a good thing, it keeps you sharp, on edge. Don't get me wrong, if I get the chance to put a bullet in Becca's head, I won't hesitate."

The image of Paddy O'May being shot by a mysterious woman sent a shiver through Mack. He said, "Let's go to the first location and hope Paddy's there."

Swerdlov put the car in drive and slowly pulled out into the lane

They drove in silence, both lost in their thoughts again.

Mack mulled over the fate of the man who ratted out Anna's parents to J Otis Weil. Taking the man's life sounded like a business transaction.

He raised his finger and asked, "How did you gain J Otis' trust in such a short period of time."

"Short period of time?" Swerdlov scoffed. "J Otis doesn't trust anyone so time wasn't a factor. It took me two years before he accepted me and barely at that. That includes my stint working undercover at Falcon Investments. The Managing Partner, Gregorz Pogladek is owned by the British Government and couldn't object to my hire, if you want to call it that."

"That's how you connected with J Otis?"

She nodded. "J Otis may be smart but he's a sick puppy. He can't control himself around teenage girls as young as thirteen and fourteen. I had a picture of a beautiful young girl on my desk. A girl I'd never met. She could pass as my little sister. The few times J Otis came into my office, he peppered me with questions about her. When I let it slip she was my youngest sister, he repeatedly invited both of us to Moscow. I finally had to promise to bring her."

"Smart, use his weakness against him."

"I used both his weaknesses, young girls and his obsession to have you killed."

Out of the blue, Mack asked, "For what agency do you work?"

Swerdlov chuckled and said, "To quote Dr. Franklyn in the Hounds of Baskerville, 'I would love to tell you, but then, of course, I'd have to kill you.'"

"That's from Top Gun."

Swerdlov shook her head in mock disgust. "Americans."

Swerdlov slowed the car and pointed out the windshield. "That strip mall up on the right is the first location from Nimesh. Let's do a couple of circles to get the lay out. Keep your eyes open for any movement."

Mack followed orders and studied the windows of

the two-story, rehabbed brick building. In every window was a yellow and black 'For Let' sign.

After circling twice, they drove around to the back of the building and parked the car in an alcove, out of sight.

"We try the back door first." She reached behind the passenger seat, lifted up a black leather bag and set it on her lap. She pulled out a black pistol and handed it to Mack.

"You ever use one of these?"

Mack studied the gun. "I can handle it."

"It's a Glock with a hair trigger and there's no safety. Be very careful."

She handed Mack an extra clip and then pulled out a second Glock and inspected it.

As they approached the back door, Swerdlov quietly said, "When we go in, stay directly behind me in case we run into trouble."

Swerdlov pressed down on the handle and slowly pulled. The door inched open.

Inside, they made their way down a short, narrow hallway. At the end of the hall, they could go either left or right. Swerdlov studied both directions and pointed to the right.

Mack stayed two steps behind her scanning everything around him.

Noises up ahead stopped them in their tracks. It sounded like a rough scraping followed by a metal creak. Music floated in the background.

Swerdlov moved silently up the hall, hugging the wall. Mack stayed close behind.

At the corner, Swerdlov glanced back at Mack and mouthed, "Stay here." She stepped around the corner with the Glock in front of her, cradled in her hands.

Mack leaned his head around the corner. Swerdlov moved like a cat about to pounce on a mouse.

Mack moved around the corner. He stood in a foyer with a large security desk directly in the center. A security guard wearing a khaki uniform leaned back in his chair, dozing. His feet rested on the desk and the radio played smooth jazz.

Swerdlov strolled over and slapped the guard's feet off the desk. He bolted upright. "What the fuck," he said, blinking repeatedly.

"Shut up and sit down," Swerdlov ordered.

The guard dropped back into his chair. As sweat droplets formed on his brow, he seemed hypnotized by Swerdlov.

"I have some questions for you," Swerdlov said.

The guard nodded nervously.

"What is this place?"

"It's a shopping mall or at least that what it wants to be."

"Who owns it?"

"I have no idea. I get my assignments from the my manager at my security company."

"Did you have any visitors within the last couple of hours?"

The guard nodded.

"Well, tell me about them."

"I didn't really see them. My supervisor called and said the owner or his manager would be here. While he was here, my boss ordered me to remain at my desk, this desk."

"You didn't see anything?"

The guard finally took his eyes off Swerdlov and looked over to Mack, desperate for his help.

Mack said, "What did you see?"

The guard flicked his head to his left. "At that end of the mall, a white van pulled up. A couple seconds later, some guy in a dark suit came out with a duffel bag and threw it in the back of the van. The van drove off and I never saw the suit again."

Swerdlov ripped the phone cord from the wall then leaned down with a smile on her face. "You did good. We were never here." She stood back up and glared at him. "You understand?"

The guard wiped the sweat from his forehead while nodding like a bobble head doll.

Swerdlov moved close to him and put her hand on his shoulder. "Good, I'd hate to have to come back." She gently tapped his crotch with the barrel of her gun.

The guard gingerly squeezed his legs together. "Thank you?" he said meekly.

§

CHAPTER 17

Swerdlov handed Mack her Glock and pointed to the floorboard. "Keep them out of sight but within reach," she said as she started the car.

She backed the car out of the alcove. Before she shifted the car into drive, Mack said, "You were a little rough on the security guard."

"I had to put the fear of God in him. If he calls anybody we're in danger, you, me and O'May."

"Is that why you ripped the phone from the wall?"

"That was for show. The man had a mobile phone in his pocket. He'll think long and hard about using it. By then, O'May should be out of danger and we can prepare to take down Becca and J Otis."

Mack sat quietly, deep in thought. Something nagged at him. Paddy disappears in what looks like an abduction in an office-building men's room. How did the kidnappers know he would be in there? Even stranger was the ransom call on Paddy's phone. Was it a coincidence that I had it? Did that lead to my abduction coming out of the workshop?

Mack scratched the back of his head. Someone had to know Paddy would be at the closing and not at his workshop. If J Otis was running the show from Moscow, and that's a big if, he had to have someone in Dublin.

He looked over at Swerdlov. If she were working with J Otis, why would she say she was using me? Wouldn't I already be dead? Something didn't fit."

Mack shook his head. Ray Gunn would not be involved if she was working with J Otis.

"Why are you shaking your head, Billy?"

Mack glanced over at her and saw her glaring at him.

"Watch the road," Mack said.

She turned her eyes to the front. "Why are you shaking your head?" she repeated.

"I've been mulling over the series of events since

Paddy disappeared."

"Events?"

Mack repeated his concerns and when he finished, said, "Something doesn't add up."

"In my world, things rarely add up. But, I'm happy you're thinking like an operative."

Mack tried to smile but failed.

Swerdlov sensed Mack's unease. "Do you trust me? I need you to trust me."

When Mack didn't answer quickly enough, she said, "Do you trust Ray Gunn?"

"With my life."

"Good, and Ray trusts me. If he didn't, I wouldn't be here with you. Deep inside, you know that but if you want, call him."

Mack thought hard about calling Ray Gunn.

While he stared at the building passing by, he felt the tension filling the car. "No need to make that call."

"Thank you. Ray has all the confidence in the world in you. That being said, we are likely to run into danger.

We are on the same team and need to have each other's backs."

"I'm good. Let's go get Paddy." Mack sat up straighter in his seat.

"I have one piece of advice. If the situation gets out of control, let your instincts take over. Don't think... react. You hesitate and you end up horizontal."

Mack made it a habit to let his instincts take over. He learned to do that in baseball. But, the pitcher was only throwing a baseball at you, not pointing a loaded gun.

He glanced at map on the phone screen. He noticed they were in Ballymun, the working class section of Dublin and where Paddy was born and raised.

They drove past buildings well along in years and in need of repair. Three young men wearing black tracksuits and white Adidas shoes with black stripes down the side leaned against a concrete wall smoking. As they drove by, the man in the center, the smallest of the three, flicked his cigarette at the car then looked at Mack and gave him the finger.

Three blocks on, Swerdlov pulled the car over to the curb and killed the engine.

"The second location is the two-story building at the

end of the next block on the right side of the road. It looks like an abandoned factory. Before we go in, we get a feel for the situation and determine our approach."

"I prefer the Bruce Willis approach. We barrel the car into the building and come out shooting."

"Next time, I'll bring Bruce Willis and we can do it your way. Right now, the best thing is to go in unnoticed and come out unnoticed... with O'May."

Mack reached down and retrieved the Glocks off the floorboard. He handed one to Swerdlov. She studied it and handed it back to him. "This is yours."

Mack lifted both pistols to compare the weight and noticed her Glock was heavier.

She realized what he was doing and said, "Mine has a modified, larger clip."

Mack handed her the heavier gun. "How are we doing this?"

"You stroll up the front side of the building from the other side of the street, go a block or two up and then stroll back down on building side of the street. I'll recon the back. We meet back here and figure out our approach."

Mack grabbed the door handle and started to pull.

"Make it look like you're going somewhere with a purpose. On the way back, look like you're in no hurry."

"Got it, I act like I live around here."

"Be back here in ten minutes," Swerdlov said. She took the phone from the cradle and placed it underneath the drivers seat.

Out on the street, Mack removed his tie and tossed it in the backseat. He buttoned his jacket and unbuttoned his shirt collar. He partially un-tucked his shirt and checked himself in the reflection from the car window. This was a working class neighborhood and he had to fit in as best he could. When he looked up, Swerdlov was gone.

§

CHAPTER 18

Mack walked up the wide sidewalk with a purpose in his step. He kept is eyes forward until he reached the abandoned factory. Half the factory was under renovation but there were no workers anywhere to be seen.

A large square banner of a simulated photo depicting the building after renovation hung from a second floor balcony. It reflected a beautiful sunny day in the picture with BEOGA SAIBHIR DEVELOPMENT stamped across the top of the banner in big black letters.

In each ground floor window, there were yellow and black 'For Let' signs.

Mack cruised up the street, walking two blocks past the building. He stood outside a small Indian restaurant pretending to read the menu in the window. He looked into the restaurant and saw a man wearing a Notre Dame baseball cap sitting alone at a table. It was too dark to make out his face. He took a step toward the door when the man stood. Mack let out a sigh of relief. The man was short and wearing a leather biker's jacket.

He chastised himself for reacting as if he'd seen a ghost before he knew the situation then crossed the street and headed back to the car. When he reached the old factory, he stopped, looked around then down at his watch. He acted like a man deciding what to do. He looked around as if uncertain what he needed to do. From what little he could see inside the factory, it was dark and empty.

He continued his walk back to the car, glancing into each window as he strolled by. If O'May was inside, he wasn't in the front part of the building.

Mack returned to the car three minutes early. He leaned against the trunk to wait for Swerdlov.

The three men who were standing on the corner a few blocks back walked toward him. The small man who'd given him the finger led the way, smiling defiantly. He'd developed a pronounced hitch in his step as he neared the car. He stopped in front of Mack.

"What the fuck you doing in my neighborhood?"

Mack didn't reply. He kept his eyes glued to the little man.

The man stepped closer and balled his hands into fists. "I asked you a fuckin' question." He stood a foot away.

Mack's hand shot up and grabbed the little man's throat. He squeezed and lifted the man up on his toes. He saw the fear in the man's eyes.

"What?"

His friend on the left, bigger than Mack, came at him then turned. He had a huge smile as Swerdlov walked up.

Swerdlov stood in front of the man.

The big guy looked at her as if he pitied her. His right fist started to come up.

Swerdlov hit him the throat before his fist moved six inches. He dropped to his knees gasping for air.

The third man sprinted away as Mack lowered the little man. He tightened his grip around the throat and said, "Your buddy will need a doctor." He released his grip and the little man rushed over and helped the big man to his feet. As they scooted away, Mack couldn't help himself. He said, "You know smoking stunts your growth."

The little man hurried his buddy down the street without looking back.

When Mack looked at Swerdlov, she said, "And you gave me a hard time with the security guard?"

Mack had no comeback.

"Who were those men?" she asked.

"I returned early and they happened to show up."

"I'm not surprised. This is Ballymun, one of the worst parts of the city and they don't take kindly to strangers, especially foreigners."

Mack changed the subject. "I didn't see anything as I walked by except empty rooms. From what I figure, the renovation has been abandoned."

Swerdlov opened the driver's door and pulled out her black leather bag. She removed a serrated knife, zip ties, a slapjack and a baton. She expanded the baton then collapsed it. "This should do fine."

Without looking at Mack she said, "O'May is inside. There are two guards watching over him."

"How is he?" Mack asked.

Swerdlov took her time answering. "He's beat up but not broken."

She clipped the knife onto her belt, shoved the zip ties in her back pocket. She handed Mack the slapjack. "Have you ever used one of these?"

Mack lifted the slapjack. It had a round handle and a stiff rubber end shaped like a thick duck's bill.

"It's called a slapjack," Swerdlov said. "You swing that like a baton at someone's head and the hard rubber end provides more than enough power to knock them out for hours."

Mack stuck the slapjack in his back pocket. "What about my gun?"

"That's the last resort." She expanded and collapsed the baton again then handed it to Mack.

He felt the baton's weight in his hand then expanded and collapsed the baton. "What's the plan?" he asked.

"We split up the guards. You position yourself at this end of the building. When I'm in place at the other end, I will signal you to break the glass on the door. Make as much noise as you can, we want one of the guards to come check it out. As soon as you break the glass, slip inside and you'll find a couple of aisles where you can wait until the guard passes by. As soon as he passes you, hit him in the back of the head with the slapjack. He'll drop like a rock. After he's down, remove his weapon and toss it away then come down to my end of the building. We'll have two on one with the other guard. Then it's easy peasy from there. We usher O'May out the back door and to the car."

They crossed the street and split up. Mack stood by the factory door as Swerdlov made her way to the far end. He expanded the baton and waited.

She waved and Mack swung the baton like he'd swung for the fences in his baseball days. The window shattered so loudly it hurt Mack's ears. He dropped the baton then reached through the broken window and opened the door. He hurried inside and ducked into the second aisle.

He heard the sound of footsteps running. The steps slowed as they approached.

The guard's focus concentrated on the broken glass spewed across the concrete floor. He passed Mack and came to a standstill. In his hand was a small pistol.

Mack stepped out and whacked the guard in the back of the head then cringed from the pain shooting from his ribs.

The guard grunted as he teetered then fell face first into the shattered glass.

Mack took the pistol from the guard's hand and tossed to the other end of the aisle. He turned and hurried to the far side of the building staying on the balls of his feet to reduce noise. He came to the end to find Swerdlov squatting behind a metal counter.

She gestured with her head for Mack to look over toward the left.

The other guard and the smaller kidnapper who manhandled Paddy O'May and tossed him into the white van. O'May was more dead weight than resistance.

A slender blonde in black pants, black knee-high boots and a tight, long sleeve black shirt stood in the delivery entrance a few feet in front of the van. Mack figured her to be five-four without her boots on. In her right hand she held a sleek black pistol with an aerated suppressor attached to the barrel.

The kidnapper gave O'May a hard shove into the van then climbed in after him. He slid the door closed from the inside.

The woman walked over to the driver side door. She moved efficiently and precisely, no motion wasted.

The guard opened the driver's door and smiled as he held it open for her.

The guard's smile vanished when she raised the pistol and shot him in the forehead. He dropped to his knees then fell over backward.

The woman climbed in and drove the van out onto the street, turned left and sped away.

Swerdlov waited until the van was gone then walked over to the dead guard. Mack quickly caught up.

"That was brutal," he said.

"That was Becca."

§

CHAPTER 19

Mack and Swerdlov stood over the dead security guard. Blood leaked from a hole the size of a dime in the middle of his forehead. His eyes were wide open, still in a state of surprise.

It bothered Mack that the dead man stared up as if he were alive. He bent down and closed the eyes. Touching a dead man bothered Mack. It wasn't proper. As he stood, he unconsciously wiped his hand on his pant leg.

Swerdlov wasn't paying attention to Mack. She stood paralyzed in thought, staring out at the street.

Mack stepped back from the body. He waited for Swerdlov to say something. She didn't.

She expelled an exasperating exhale. Mack took that as a cue and said, "That sounds like a sigh of defeat."

Swerdlov continued to study the street.

Mack walked over to her. "Like you said, all plans go awry."

That broke her concentration. She said, "I know what I said. I'm figuring out our options."

"While you're doing that, I recommend we close the garage door and get the hell out of here. We don't need to be found next to a dead body."

Swerdlov hastily gestured for Mack to close the delivery door then spun around and headed to the back.

Mack reached up for the thick rope hanging down, grabbed the fat knot and pulled the garage door to the floor. He twisted the handle, tested the door then turned and ran after Swerdlov.

At the back door, she said, "We wait until we get to the car to talk."

On the way, Mack picked up the baton lying among the glass shards in front of the open door.

Mack climbed into the passenger's seat, gently placed the Glock on the floor. He held up the baton and slapjack for Swerdlov to take.

She was again stuck in thought, her thumb pressed against her chin.

Mack dropped the baton and slapjack next to the Glock and said, "We should still be able to track the kidnapper with Nimesh's program."

She reached under the seat for her phone and clicked it into the cradle. The GPS program had quit. "Battery's low," she said. "There's a charger in the glove box. It plugs directly into the phone."

As soon as Mack plugged in the phone, Swerdlov tapped the screen and punched in a number. She hit the speaker button and waited.

"What's up?" Ray Gunn's voice bellowed through the car.

"We've hit a bump," Swerdlov answered. "We found O'May but arrived too late. The abductors took him out just as we arrived."

"That's more than a bump." Gunn sounded disappointed.

Mack realized what Gunn must be thinking and quickly added, "She means taken away, not taken out.

He's alive but back on the move."

"That's not the worst of it," Swerdlov added. "Becca now has him. She and one of the kidnappers took him away in a white van."

"Stay on the line," Gunn said. "I'm connecting Nimesh to our call."

After a few clicks, Nimesh came on. He said, "Keep talking while I get the programs back up."

Gunn updated Nimesh on the situation then said, "Becca went through customs with diplomatic immunity. That means J Otis is determined to kill two birds with one Becca. Sorry Billy but nothing will happen to you, I promise."

"Let's focus on finding Paddy."

"Agreed. I'll see what I can find out about J Otis being in Dublin."

After an uncomfortable pause, Mack asked, "What's the status of the closing?"

"We're still waiting for wire transfers to be confirmed. Steve Gray and Pius Malloy spoke with each investor and postponed the dinner until tomorrow. Malloy subtly blamed Pogladek and the Frenchman

LeBeau for the delay without making it a big deal."

Swerdlov said, "Ray, you'll need to keep Pogladek busy. We don't want him talking with J Otis while he's in Dublin. At least until we figure out how we can use him."

"Great minds think alike. I'll have Gray handle him."

"A couple of things are really nagging at me and I gotta believe they're key to Paddy's fate," Mack said.

"Talk to me," Gunn replied.

"First, how did the kidnappers know Paddy would be in the restroom, or for that matter, even at the closing knowing he can't handle crowds? Second, beside revenge against me, why is J Otis in Dublin? It means he's involved in Paddy's kidnapping — why? Third, was Becca, a world class assassin brought in to kill me, kill Paddy or kill both of us?"

Nimesh added, "Why do the kidnappers seem to be one step ahead?"

"Great questions all," Gunn said. "To get the answers, we need to connect the dots, look for any links or coincidences. Remember, any speculation needs to end up with a firm connection."

"Paddy's life depends on us finding answers," Mack

added.

"Yours does as well Billy," Swerdlov added.

Nimesh cut in, "The GPS is up and running. It looks like the van is in Glasnevin Cemetery, in the far northwest corner."

"Let's go, before they bury Paddy," Mack said.

Swerdlov nervously shifted in her seat. "Ray, did you meet Detective Dillon when she arrived?"

"Yes, she's a good cop. I thought I would have a difficult time keeping her from questioning all the investors but she didn't argue. Why?"

"I'll fill you in when we have more time. I can tell you one thing. Dillon is good people. Please call her and tell her there's a body as wall as an unconscious guard at the second location? The dead body is the handiwork of Becca."

"Done. Now go get Paddy."

"Contact me if you need anything," Nimesh added.

Swerdlov started the engine. "Let's go get Paddy," she said with grit and determination, as if the phone call sparked her energy.

"Drive past the factory first. I want to check something. Do you have pen and paper?"

"In the glove box."

Swerdlov slowed as they passed the factory.

Mack flipped open the small notebook in his hand, wrote out the phone number on the For Let signs and then scribbled down every word on the large colorful banner.

He noticed Swerdlov looking at him with a perplexed look. He said, "Hey, there could be a connection to something."

"I didn't say anything."

"Where's this cemetery?" Mack said.

"Straight south of here, we're on Ballymun Road and we stay on this route until we turn right on Finglas Road which leads us to the cemetery."

"They will see us coming."

"Not if we drive past the cemetery and come in from the northwest." She tapped the phone and a satellite photo came on the screen. She pointed to the northwest corner of the cemetery. "See those trees? That's our cover."

They turned right and were driving west on Finglas Road. Mack eyed the cemetery up ahead.

Out of the blue, he asked, "How do you think the kidnappers knew where Paddy was?"

Swerdlov thought about her answer.

"I can only think of three possibilities. They either followed him there, someone on the inside gave him up, or it was pure luck. In my business I never believe in luck."

"What about Pogladek? He has the connection to J Otis. It's either him or someone inside the conference room who are the most likely."

"Highly doubtful since we own him and his family," Swerdlov said. "If he betrays us, he'll never see his wife and kids again and he knows that."

"Well then... give me a possibility."

"I won't speculate, at least not yet."

Swerdlov lifted her hand for Mack to stay quiet. She cut the engine and rolled the car to a stop behind a clump of trees. She whispered, "You see anything?"

Mack scanned the deserted cemetery.

"The GPS indicates they are here," Swerdlov said.

Mack took the pistol off the floor and climbed out of the car. He stayed behind the trees as he approached the gravestones.

Swerdlov joined him and they walked into the cemetery.

"Up there on the right, behind the tall black tombstone with the cross on top is a pair of black shoes, toes down," Mack said.

"I'll go around left and you approach from the right, Billy."

Mack moved swiftly between tombstones, using them as cover. The low gray clouds muted the daylight easing Mack's fear of being watched. He prayed the shoes didn't belong to Paddy.

He and Swerdlov arrived at the tall black tombstone at the same time.

Lying face down in the grass was the other kidnapper. Mack rolled him over and immediately wiped his hand on his pant leg. The kidnapper had a hole the size of a dime in the center of his forehead. His eyes were tightly closed. He knew what was coming.

Mack felt a vibration in his front pant pocket. He pulled out O'May's phone and stared at it. He'd forgotten he still had it.

The caller ID read: UNKNOWN.

§

CHAPTER 20

Mack slowly brought the phone to his ear. He noticed Swerdlov looking suspiciously at him. He shrugged to let her know he had no idea why the phone rang. He broke eye contact and said, "Billy Mack."

"You should answer the phone, 'Billy the loser Mack' because you're a washed up baseball player and a third-rate investment manager."

"Nice to talk to you as well, J Otis." Mack replied. He thought of Paddy O'May and gave Swerdlov a hapless grin. He tapped the speaker button so she could listen.

"You had one job to do to save your defective little buddy and-"

"He's ten times the man you think you are, J Otis."

"Shut the fuck up... prick. I know what you did with the wire transfer. I know you better than you know yourself. Always remember that. You may have fooled some people but not me. I only live by a few rules and one of them is 'Try and fool me once, shame on you, you're dead.' Now, if you want your little buddy to see tomorrow, you go back to the bank and initiate the wire transfer."

Mack glanced down at his watch. "The bank's closed."

He heard J Otis breathing heavily then the phone went completely silent.

Mack pressed the phone against his chest. "I think he hung up."

Swerdlov shook her head. "He's not alone. He's on mute while they figure out what they'll do."

Mack held the phone out in front of him.

Swerdlov turned in a deliberate circle, surveying the cemetery. Something caught her eye. She slowed to a stop, exhaled and resumed turning.

J Otis came back on the line. "At nine o'clock tomorrow morning the money will be in the account sent to your phone."

"Since you know me better than I know myself, you know I'm not going to do that. Once the money is in the account, Paddy is as good as dead. But, I'm still around and that drives you crazy."

"You think too highly of yourself."

Mack laughed easily knowing it would set off J Otis.

"Fuck you Mack. You have until nine tomorrow morning."

"Here's how it's going down, J Otis. The ten million will be ready to go at nine tomorrow. Once Paddy is let go and I confirm he's safe, I will contact the bank with the approval password but only after I confirm Paddy is out of danger."

Muffled voices came through the phone. Swerdlov come closer and cocked her ear. Mack tried to decipher the faint voices.

J Otis' voice then came through clearly. "You will be sent instructions tomorrow morning with a time and a place for you and you alone to be. Be ready to go as soon as you get the instructions."

The connection ended.

"I'm coming along," Swerdlov said.

Mack didn't like that idea. He opened his mouth to argue then held his tongue and thought about his reply. She was an asset, trained to deal with situations like this.

At the end of the row of gravestones, a man wearing a dark gray overcoat came walking toward him. Mack turned to get a better look. The man stopped when he saw Mack. He looked surprised. He adjusted the lapels then stuck his hands into both pockets. He turned and looked behind him.

His coat extended to his ankles. A tightly wrapped black scarf hid his neck. He stood motionless like a cat deciding what to do.

A small woman, slightly hunched over, came around a gravestone. She wore a heavy black coat that grazed the ground. She looked at Mack and smiled innocently. Mack realized the couple was old enough to be his parents.

"They're fine, Billy," Swerdlov said. "I saw them earlier standing in front of a grave. Before they walked away, they both made the sign of the cross."

"Why didn't you say something earlier?"

"Because they're just an old couple visiting a grave."

The woman gasped when she saw the dead body and hastily covered her mouth with her hand. She immediately took the man's elbow and pulled. As he turned the man shook his head pleading with Mack to leave them be. Mack felt guilty as he watched them hurry away.

"We best go before they call the police," Mack said.

"At the pace they're moving, we have time."

"If they have a cell phone, they'll be calling as soon as they're out of sight."

"We don't need to worry about the police. We've done nothing wrong," Swerdlov said.

"By the time the cops figure that out, Paddy will be dead."

"You're jumpy, Billy. That's why I'm coming along to the bank and to the meet."

Mack knew she was right. He also knew he had until morning to decide. "Before we make any decisions, let's circle back with Ray Gunn. I also want to see if Nimesh can dig up some information for us."

"What kind of information?"

"Why did the kidnappers stop at the first building but didn't stay there? What did they pick up when they stopped? Why did they hold Paddy at the second building? Both buildings looked like they were being renovated but the renovation work had stopped some time ago."

"That could just be a coincidence," Swerdlov said.

"According to Ray Gunn there are no coincidences. Isn't that a rule of thumb in your business?" Mack glanced at his watch. "Let's hustle and be on the road before the cops come."

Swerdlov smiled, rolled her eyes and shook her head. "You worry too much about the police. And, yes, there usually are no coincidences but there may also be simple answers to your questions."

"If anyone can find the answers, it's Nimesh."

Swerdlov shook the car keys and said, "Let's go see Ray. You can call Nimesh on the way."

On the walk back to the car Mack called Gunn. He was still in the conference room talking to Steve Gray. Mack estimated he and Swerdlov would be there in twenty minutes.

Once they turned onto Finglas Road, Mack lifted O'May's phone in order to call Nimesh.

Nimesh's face filled the screen. His hair was dyed yellow blonde, matching the yellow frame of his glasses.

Mack was taken aback by all the yellow.

"My daughter Esha gave me the glasses for my birthday," Nimesh said in anticipation. "She likes yellow."

"What happened to your hair?"

"I lost a bet and I'm not going to waste time telling you why."

A map of Dublin popped onto the screen. Nimesh said, "Ray Gunn is right. Ray Gunn is always right. There are no coincidences. There is a connection between the-"

"Wait," Mack said, "how do you know what we've been talking about?"

"I stayed on your phone after our conversation with Ray."

Mack looked over at Swerdlov.

She said, "Don't look surprised, Billy. Your government and mine can turn on any phone or computer without the user knowing it. Nimesh developed the technology and provided it to both our countries."

Nimesh said, "Don't worry Billy, I'll never turn on

your phone without first telling you."

"You just did."

"No, this is Paddy O'May's phone."

"A distinction without a difference."

"Welcome to our world," Swerdlov said.

"See the three red pins on the map? They represent the two buildings where the phone pinged and the third is a residential location on the outskirts of Dublin. Two of the properties are currently owned by Beoga Saibher Development."

"Are they the two buildings we just left?" Mack asked.

"No, the empty office building and the residential property are owned by the development company."

"What about the abandoned factory where Paddy was being held? Is there a connection?"

Mack stared at the map on the screen waiting for Nimesh to answer. The longer the silence went on, the tighter he squeezed to phone.

Nimesh finally said, "Yes, there is a connection but I need to dig into it more." Nimesh's hesitant tone told

Mack not to say anything just yet.

"Tell us what you know so far. We can't operate in the dark," Swerdlov said.

After a brief hesitation, Nimesh said, "The abandoned factory is owned by Pius Malloy."

§

CHAPTER 21

"The factory is owned by Puis Malloy? That can't be true," Mack yelled into the phone. That piece of information hit him like a hard slap in the face. "He's flat broke."

"I'm only telling you how it's listed in the Property Registration Authority and the Registry of Deeds. I was surprised as you are so I double-checked. He bought the property a month ago." Nimesh's voice was resolute.

"Son of a bitch," Mack whispered.

"You can say that again," Nimesh said. "Here's the connection. He bought the property at a deep discount from Beoga Saibher Development."

"Define deep discount."

"He bought the factory for a hundred Euros. However, the property had a multitude of liens against it ranging from property taxes to unpaid bills. As soon as the property changed hands, the liens all went away. I'm calculating the exact amount, but that'll take time. I estimate it to be at least a half million Euros."

"What does that tell us about the development company?"

"It's shady at best. It's incorporated in Malta as a subsidiary of an offshore company registered in Panama."

Mack chuckled and said, "Based on my experience, incorporating in Panama is done for one reason and one reason only, secrecy. You won't find any individual names associated with either company unless we can identify the firm in Panama that registered the company and that's iffy." Mack raised and wiggled his finger. "But, we can get the information we need right here in Dublin."

"And he's sitting in the conference room," Swerdlov added.

"Nimesh, call Ray and tell him we are on our way and to keep Pius busy until we get there. Nobody say a word to Malloy about anything."

Swerdlov weaved through the stop-and-go traffic. She only took her foot off the gas pedal when she approached a red light or stop sign, treating them like yield signs. Mack kept a firm grip on the handle above his head and tried to block out the stinging pain in his ribcage. Neither said a word for ten minutes.

As he blankly stared out the windshield, the same thought reverberated inside his head and it bugged him. He couldn't shake the thought and finally broke his white-knuckled silence, "I can't believe I trusted him."

Swerdlov paused before she replied. She tapped the steering wheel and said, "It looks bad but, and I say this from experience, don't jump to conclusions. We don't have all the information."

Mack wasn't paying attention to her. "Where the hell did he get the money? He couldn't walk into a bank and ask for it."

Swerdlov looked over at Mack and ran through a red light. In the middle of the intersection she swerved and narrowly missed the back tire of a motorcycle. Mack didn't notice.

The motorcyclist sped away holding up his middle finger.

The closer they got to the conference center and to Pius Malloy, the more Mack's anger swelled.

Swerdlov sensed his anger. "Calm down, going in all enraged won't help us and definitely won't help us find Paddy. Confront Malloy objectively... at least at first."

"I trusted him," Mack said as if he made a grave mistake. "If they hurt Paddy-"

"Keep your wits about you," Swerdlov said firmly, cutting Mack off. "Malloy doesn't know we know. If you go at him hard, he'll dummy up. Should we need someone to play bad cop, let it be Ray Gunn. He knows how to play the game. He'll either put the fear of God in him or get Malloy to want to tell us."

Mack worked to calm himself. Gunn can get people to talk just by the way he looks at them.

When Swerdlov turned into the parking lot, his blood began to boil again. He sucked in a soothing breath to slow his heart down.

Swerdlov stopped the car directly in front of the entrance then placed her hand firmly on Mack's thigh and said, "Relax, you're riled up based on only one piece of information. Play this out."

In the short walk it took to get to the front doors,

Mack calmed himself. He was determined to be rational when he confronted Malloy - at least at first.

He followed Swerdlov inside the building and up the stairs.

At the conference room door, Swerdlov reached for the handle then turned and gave Mack a stern look. He got the message.

She pushed open the door and walked in. Mack kept close on her heels.

Sitting at the large conference table across the room were Ray Gunn, Steve Gray and Pius Malloy. They were huddled at the left end of the long table. Gunn faced them while Malloy sat with his back to them. Gray sat at the end of the table facing both and was doing the talking.

Gunn nodded nearly imperceptibly when he saw Mack and Swerdlov approaching. As they neared, he stood.

Malloy turned and smiled at Mack as he stood.

Mack looked past Malloy to see Gunn decisively wagging his finger and shaking his head.

Mack got the message and forced a smile. His eyes however said something different.

Malloy picked up the mixed message and furrowed his brow. His shoulders slumped and he said, "Did something happen to Paddy. Please tell me no." He looked like he was about to cry.

Swerdlov stepped in between. "Sit down, Pius. When we saw him he was alive but a little beat up. We need to ask you some questions."

"You saw him? Is he on his way?" Malloy looked over at the conference room door as if he expected O'May to walk through it.

"He's been abducted but we briefly caught a glimpse of him. The kidnappers took him away just as we arrived," Swerdlov said. She gently maneuvered Malloy back down into his chair. "In order to find him, we need to ask you a few questions." She sensed Mack was about to interrupt and held up her hand.

Malloy glanced at Mack and then at Gunn with a look of anguish, uncertainty and fear. "Abducted?"

Gunn nodded and said, "We are on it. Your answers will determine if Paddy lives or dies."

§

CHAPTER 22

"I'm confused," Malloy said. He turned to Steve Gray. "Do you know what's going on?"

Gray soberly stared at Malloy then shrugged his shoulders. "Sorry."

Mack took a step toward Malloy. "Paddy-"

Swerdlov jabbed her palm against Mack's chest and pushed him back. She gave him a look that said shut up and let me handle this.

Mack stepped back then walked around the table and stood next to Gunn. His eyes never left Malloy.

"Can someone please tell me what's going on?" Malloy's voice trembled and jumped an octave.

Swerdlov sat next to Malloy in order to calm him down. Her body language suggested she was on Malloy's side.

"Pius, I'm about to tell you what we've discovered about Paddy and why it looks bad for you. I don't want you to interrupt me. That is a sign of guilt. After I finish, you can ask us any questions or clarify or correct anything I've said, understand?"

Malloy slumped in his chair, closed his eyes and nodded.

Swerdlov adjusted her sitting position and waited for Malloy to open his eyes and look at her.

She said, "I'm going to start at the beginning. Your partner was taken from here earlier today... Abducted is the right word. A white van transported him to an abandoned building where a man in a suit brought out some kind of bag and threw it in the back of the van. The man then disappeared. The van proceeded to an abandoned factory in Ballymun."

Malloy sat up straight when Swerdlov said 'Ballymun.'

Swerdlov continued, "At this abandoned factory, there were two armed guards and a killer for hire. We disabled one guard and went to rescue Paddy. By the time we got there, the guard had already forced Paddy back into the van. That's when the killer for hire shot the other guard between the eyes and drove away. Are you following me?"

Malloy nodded anxiously.

Swerdlov smiled easily and said, "We don't think we have much time to rescue Paddy. We have some information that seems useful and have some of the best people we know working on it, including a top detective with the Guards." Swerdlov paused for affect. "Our people have come across information that leads us to believe the killer for hire has multiple targets - Paddy 0'May, Billy Mack and you."

Her lie was meant to unsettle Malloy. It worked.

Malloy sat frozen, his eyes looking at nothing.

Gunn placed his palms on the table and leaned in. He calmly said, "Pius, do you have any questions or can you provide us with any information we don't have?"

Malloy shook himself out of his daze. He looked at each person around the table. He waited until he caught eyes with Mack. "Is this abandoned factory on Shangan Road, just off Ballymun Road?" Malloy asked, his tone stronger, more confident.

Mack glanced at Swerdlov and she nodded.

"That's the one."

"We own that building."

"You mean you own that building." Mack said harshly.

"No, Paddy and I own the building. I bought it a couple of months back. We were offered too good a deal to pass up and we had to move fast. We bought the building in my name but Paddy and I have a written contract naming us joint owners. In the contract there is a provision mandating us to sell the building to our company at the price we paid once this deal is closed. The contract is signed by Paddy, me and Kieran Sweeney, who signed on behalf of The Celtic Tiger. The original copies are with a lawyer friend of ours who drafted it."

"How come you never told us this?" Mack asked.

"Because it wasn't your decision. It was a management decision. The low price made it a great deal and we had to act fast. It was a great deal even after paying off the debt to release the liens on the property." He grinned at Mack. "In case it slipped your mind, we need a factory to build our engines."

The sarcasm was not lost on Mack. "Did you look at any other properties?" As soon as Mack asked the question, he knew the answer.

"When you go to buy a car and find exactly what you want at a fantastic deal, do you keep looking, Billy?"

Malloy didn't wait for Mack to answer. "Besides, the factory is in Ballymun, a shite part of town where Paddy grew up. It is more important than you know for him to bring jobs to the people, the poor people, he's known his entire life."

Swerdlov turned Malloy's chair so he faced her. "Who did you buy the property from?"

"A real estate development company. Apparently, they were planning on developing it into some kind of an apartment and shopping complex but gave up on it."

"How did you learn about the property?"

"Paddy sister, Claire Donovan came to us saying she had perfect location for our factory. You met her earlier today."

"Did she own the building?"

Malloy shook his head. "She acted as our agent and represented us in the negotiations. She handled all the paperwork with the seller. All we had to do was sign. Part of the deal was that we paid the agent fees... both buyer and seller. Because it was such a great price, we didn't object."

"I thought she owned some kind of import company that sold tiger urine?" Mack asked.

Malloy laughed. "She does and sells that stuff to self-important social skeletons who believe it tightens their skin. They are her kind of people."

Malloy smiled at his joke then added, "She and her husband have a number of other companies. They brag about them every chance they get."

On the other side of the room, Gregorz Pogladek and Pierre Le Beau walked into the room and stood just inside the door with their hands on their hips. Their ties were casually loosened but from the look on their faces, they were unhappy.

§

CHAPTER 23

When Mack saw Pogladek and LeBeau standing together, he nudged Ray Gunn and whispered, "What the hell are they doing here?"

"We left them alone too long," Gunn answered quietly. "Pogladek is shrewd. He knows something is wrong and he's riled up LeBeau. They've both been peppering me with questions either about Paddy or about the technology and demanding copies of the schematics. Pogladek is being diplomatic, using LeBeau to play bad cop."

"Any suggestions?"

Gunn rubbed his baldhead in thought. He looked keenly over at Pogladek and LeBeau. "Separate them and figure out a way to put a wedge between them," he said, his voice even softer. "You talk to LeBeau, We know he's clean. Tell him there may be a problem with the exclusivity agreement for the European recharging business but let him know you want to work it out. Anna can deal with Pogladek and work the J Otis angle. He's scared shitless of her and may tell us something he doesn't even know he knows."

Swerdlov heard what Gunn had said and stood up. She leaned down and in, face-to-face with Malloy and said, "Stay here and keep a smile plastered on your face."

By the time she turned around, Mack was at her side. They strolled over to Pogladek and LeBeau.

Mack gripped LeBeau by the elbow and turned him toward the door. He said, "Pierre, I'm glad you're here. Something has come up last minute and I want to talk to you about it." Mack released his grip on LeBeau's elbow. "Let's take a walk. I need to stretch my legs."

"What is zeees last-meenute some-sing?" LeBeau asked, his French accent more pronounced due to increased stress.

"Let's circle the floor, get the blood flowing." As they started walking, Mack had to think quickly. He remembered the issues that had been holding up the exclusivity agreement granted to LeBeau and his investors before Ray Gunn resolved them. One key issue popped into his mind.

"You and your biggest investor, Total Service, were granted an exclusive ten-year agreement to provide the recharging stations and equipment throughout the European Union."

"Yes, eees there a problem?"

"An unforeseen issues has arisen. It relates to Great Britain. We've learned that any EU-wide contracts signed when Britain was with the EU will not be valid in Britain once they leave the EU. Unfortunately, we cannot have a contract for Britain ready for you to sign for at least a month."

"Zeees eees a problem for us. Zeee deal eees now much deeferant."

LeBeau replied exactly as Mack expected. He looked up as if he were pondering all available options. He let a smile grow on his face and looked back down. "If you want to void the exclusivity deal, that's fine. We can both walk away. If you also then want to back out of the investment all together, that's fine as well. My firm and some of the other investors will cover your commitment. That's not how I want to proceed. I want you in the deal."

Le Beau visibly relaxed and his English improved. "No, no, I want to stay eeen as well but I must tell you I will have a big problem with my investor if we do not have recharging beesness."

Mack rubbed his chin. "There is one option that keeps your deal in place. It's legally binding but not a contract."

"What is it?" LeBeau asked.

"The contract for the EU stays in place and The Celtic Horse provides a letter granting you the exclusive rights to Great Britain under an agreement to be drafted to fit British law. British courts have ruled such a letter legally binding."

Le Beau nodded slowly. "Zatt ees acceptable."

"Good, Other investors were pushing me for as much as possible in case I had to divvy up your investment."

"Divvy up my investment? What is divvy?"

Mack looked at LeBeau like he had a juicy secret that he couldn't hold in any longer. "We give your shares to other investors."

LeBeau asked, "Between you and me, what other

investors want to increase their investment in your company?"

"Falcon Investments came to us a week ago. I have to believe that's why Gregorz is playing hardball. Hoping it would scare away an investor or two."

Mack fought back a smile from the stunned look on LeBeau's face.

Mack said, "Yesterday, he asked me some strange questions about Paddy O'May. They were unusual questions about Paddy's mental health like a lawyer trying to create a narrative, if you know what I mean."

Le Beau grimaced. "He is worried about O'May and that is why we wants the technology as collateral. He's been pushing me to back him up or get out of the deal. Do you think he was playing me?"

"What do you think?" Mack folded his arms across his chest and gave LeBeau a look that said you know the answer. "Gregorz also asked me about the status of our agreement to grant you the exclusive rights to the charging station." Mack flicked his eyebrows up.

"I will stay in the deal as we have now agreed with letter for Britain."

"Good decision." Mack pointed his finger at LeBeau.

"This is between you and me, Pierre. Gregorz confided in me like I just did with you."

"After I have the letter, I will authorize the wire transfer. You will have our money tomorrow morning."

"It's probably better that you avoid Gregorz and anyone from Falcon Investments until the closing dinner."

"I think you are right."

Mack patted LeBeau on the shoulder. "I will have Steve Gray draft the letter and have it delivered to your hotel within the hour. If you have changes, call Steve. Malloy can sign the letter this evening."

Mack watched LeBeau walk over to the stairs and descend. He strolled back to the conference room hoping Swerdlov had useful information from Pogladek.

Walking in he saw Swerdlov and Gunn standing in the corner away from Malloy and Gray. They were locked in an intense discussion.

He signaled he'll be right there and marched over to Gray and Malloy still sitting at the table. He told them about the letter to be drafted. When Gray nodded his understanding, Mack hurried over to Swerdlov and Gunn.

As he approached, Swerdlov and Gunn turned to face him, the seriousness of their discussion still evident on their faces.

Before Mack reached them, Gunn said, "Did LeBeau have anything interesting to say?"

"Yes, even though he didn't know it." He explained how he used pretext of the problem with the exclusivity arrangement that led LeBeau into believing he was being played by Pogladek into getting out of the deal.

"LeBeau mentioned Pogladek is pressing him hard to back him up on the demand to use the technology as security."

"There's a good reason for that," Swerdlov said. "One of Pogladek's largest investors in Falcon recently sold half their fund investment to the Chinese government. They along with his Russian investors are demanding he provide them with the technology."

"It'll never happen."

"Pogladek is scared. The Chinese are threatening him."

"I thought MI6 owned him?"

Those words made Swerdlov uncomfortably shift her feet. "Owning someone is different from protecting someone. His value as an asset is not high enough to justify the cost of protection."

"Pogladek made his own bed," Gunn said coldly. "We use him to extricate Paddy. After that, he is not our concern."

Swerdlov didn't like him expunging one of her assets but didn't contradict Gunn, an unwritten rule in her world. "Gregorz was very forthcoming," she said hoping it would eventually help Pogladek. "He had no idea of Paddy's abduction and claimed to be as shocked as we were. I believe him. He claimed he was unwittingly used by J Otis, the Russian President and the Chinese."

"Unwittingly? Pogladek?" Mack nearly laughed aloud. "The man is pleading stupidity and thinks we'll fall for it."

"Let me explain," Swerdlov countered. "When J Otis first found out about an investment in Ireland he strongly suggested Falcon Investments open an account in Dublin. Gregorz had no choice. This was before J Otis ever knew of The Celtic Horse. As soon as Gregorz opened the account, J Otis began wiring funds into the account and instructed Gregorz where to make payments to that account. When J Otis learned about the investment in The Celtic Horse and the fact that the lead investor was

Billy Mack, the account activity tripled."

"Gregorz just volunteered that information?" Mack asked skeptically.

"I've been working to bring down J Otis' sex trafficking ring for some time now and can confirm this information. Once we tracked the money, one of my colleagues confronted Gregorz letting him know he could be charged as a co-conspirator in a major international sex trafficking ring and be sent away forever. That's how we came to own him."

Knowing very little of Swerdlov's work, Mack changed the subject. "We need the transaction history of that account."

Swerdlov didn't gloat. "The account number and requisite passwords are with Nimesh and he's compiling the information as we stand here. We should have the information quickly."

"What can we expect to learn from the information?" Mack asked.

"We wait and see."

"We may not have that luxury."

"Has Nimesh ever disappointed before?"

Mack shook his head vigorously. "What else did Pogladek tell you about J Otis?"

"He knows he's in Dublin and that J Otis would contact him when needed."

"Did you let Gregorz leave?"

"I have someone keeping an eye on him."

§

CHAPTER 24

"Where's Malloy think he's going?" Gunn asked, pointing with his chin to Malloy strolling across the room.

Before anyone answered, Swerdlov marched across the room to cut him off.

Swerdlov spoke briefly to Malloy before he turned around and walked back and sat by Steve Gray.

Swerdlov strolled back to Mack and Gunn looking satisfied.

"He was going to the bathroom. At least that's what he said. I reminded him it was a crime scene and the urge went away."

Mack nervously looked at his watch. "What's taking Nimesh?"

As if on cue, Swerdlov's phone vibrated. She held it up for Mack and Gunn to see. "It's Nimesh." She brought the phone to her ear.

"Put it on speaker," Mack said.

Swerdlov shook her head and moved away from Mack and Gunn.

Mack looked at Gunn like 'what the hell?'

"There are too many ears around to put the call on speaker. She'll let us know what Nimesh has for us."

Mack shifted his feet, looked at his watch again then began walking in small circles. He stopped walking when he heard Swerdlov say, "Thanks Nims."

"Well?" Mack said impatiently.

"The account activity provided by Pogladek is very telling. The first wave of wire transfers through the account went to suspected sex traffickers thought to be affiliated with the Russian mafia. Then over the last couple months, money began moving to the accounts of Irish companies or individuals, many of which are in real estate. There were a few wire transfers to companies engaged in the import-export business."

"Did he discover any connections to The Celtic

Horse or Paddy?" Gunn asked.

"Nothing direct but he did find an account for Beoga Saibhir Development in Malta. They were the firm developing the abandoned factory where Paddy was being held... before they sold it to Malloy."

"Does Nimesh have any other information pointing to the factory or the address of the factory?" Mack asked.

"Nothing on the factory but there were three transfers totaling less than a million dollars earmarked for the purchase of a property on Pigeon House Road in Ringsend, across the street from the port. The property is a small, rundown hotel and was sold less than a month ago. Get this, the name on the account is the same as on the deed - Beoga Saibhir Development."

"The easiest way to move things, including people, in and out of this country is by water," Gunn said.

"And the best place to hide someone is a cheap hotel," Mack added.

"What are the odds Paddy is being held there?" Gunn asked.

"It's the only common thread Nimesh has come up with so far. He thinks it's highly likely Paddy is there." Swerdlov answered, "At this point, it's only conjecture.

We need to pull that thread no matter the odds."

"How are we going to pull that tread?" Mack asked.

Swerdlov watched Gunn massage his temples in thought. Sensing Mack was about to say something, she gestured with her hands for him to wait.

"We need a few more people," Gunn finally said, "people we can trust implicitly." His eyes drilled into Swerdlov's to underscore how deadly serious he was.

"I'll call Detective Dillon. She's been invaluable to my operation."

"Have her pick a place for us to meet and have her select four of her most trusted officers."

Swerdlov took a couple of steps away from Mack and called Dillon. She spoke so quietly Mack picked up only every other word.

She turned around and said, "There's a deserted parking lot near a diner on Sean Moore Road across from the docks. The hotel is a hundred meters away. From there we can access the hotel from three sides."

"We need to do some reconnaissance before we come up with a plan," Gunn said.

"Nimesh is downloading the blueprints of the hotel

and a series of images of the property from a drone that he already has up. We should have the plans by the time we get in the car."

"We need tactical gear. Ask Dillon to bring vests, assault rifles, sidearms and a variety of explosives for breaching."

"I already asked her to bring all the SWAT gear she had."

"We'll also need wire cutters, flashlights and whatever thermal energy sensors she can get her hands on."

"I have those with me. They're in the boot of my car."

Swerdlov's phone beeped simultaneously with Gunn's phone. Gunn's alert was more of a chirp.

"Nimesh," they said in unison.

Mack stood next to Swerdlov to get a good look at her screen. Swerdlov held her phone between them.

A red-brick, three-story building that resembled an old house with haphazard additions on the right side and behind popped onto the small screen. The additions to the right side and the back had only one floor. The front door was black. There were three windows in the front, one on each level. The left side of the house had the same but with a smaller window configuration. The right side and the back of the building had no windows. Centered in the back wall was a cellar door. A three-foot, red-brick wall surrounded the property.

"Do you see the black frames on the door and the windows?" Gunn asked but didn't expect an answer. "Those are new, bullet proof and bomb resistant. I hope Dillon brings the right explosives to breach those doors."

"Are we planning on blasting our way inside? Won't that endanger Paddy?"

"Do you have a better idea? If so, let us know," Swerdlov said.

"Billy, I've done this more times than I can count," Gunn said. "The blast is concussive and stuns anybody inside the house. Still, we won't make a decision on how we breach until we know more."

"I'm sorry, I'm just worried for Paddy. When we go in, please make sure no one shoots him."

A wry smile emerged on Gunn's face. He said, "We? You're not going with us."

"Yes I am."

Gunn emphatically shook his. "You're not trained in hostage rescue. We go silent as soon as we arrive and don't have the time to train you in signals communication. It's much too dangerous."

Before Mack could argue, Swerdlov put her arm around his shoulder and said, "Billy, in every operation there is a command post. Nimesh is our eye in the sky giving us a sitrep. If we lose contact him when we're in the field, you're our ears. We also need you to keep an eye on Malloy."

Mack bit his tongue. He couldn't just sit there and hope Paddy was alive.

"Ready to roll?" Swerdlov said to Gunn.

Mack watched them stroll across the room and out the door.

He looked over to Gray. "I gotta do what I gotta do," he said sullenly.

§

CHAPTER 25

While Mack waited for Gunn and Swerdlov to rendezvous with Dillon and the Guards, he thought about Nimesh's latest information. It wasn't the real estate connection that nagged at him. It was the import-export companies. If you want to move people illicitly, an import-export company is the perfect cover.

He fished O'May's phone from his pocket and called Nimesh. He didn't hide his frustration. "Hey Nims, It's the go-between calling."

"You don't sound happy with your role."

"I'm not. I've been benched. I didn't like it when I played and I don't like it now."

"We've all had to step back and play a support role

once or twice. I know that's no consolation."

"While we wait for the team to get in position, I have some a questions I want to throw at you about the latest information you uncovered."

"I'm still running queries but will give you everything I have."

"Some of the accounts receiving wire transfers were import-export companies. Were any based in Dublin?"

"Give me a minute."

Mack heard the clatter of typing. The clatter stopped then started again.

"I only have information on two so far. One company is in the town of Carrickmacross, which is a little over an hour north of Dublin. The other is just outside Dublin in County Meath. The location abuts County Dublin."

"The company in Carrickmacross seems like a long shot, given the distance from Dublin."

"I think you're right, Billy. The house is outside Carrickmacross and owned by an Australian. His name is Tim Hayden and he imports wine. Based on his travel records, he spends most of his time at his vineyard in

Australia or his villa in Switzerland."

"Why would he own a property in some out-of-the-way town in Ireland?"

"His wife is from Carrickmacross and it looks like they bought the family farm."

"Cross him off the list. What about the other company?"

"It's an importer of skincare products from the Far East... hmmmm, interesting," Nimesh said. "Digging deeper, the headquarters is located in a business park developed by, get this, Beoga Saibhir Development and sold six months ago to Tiger Products, an import-export company registered in Panama."

"Compare the address for the Panama company to the three properties from earlier today."

"It's the same address for the third property. It's zoned residential on Kribensis Manor but the addresses match."

Mack couldn't contain himself. "You can put it on the booooooard... yes."

"Come again?"

"Sorry." Mack let out a soft laugh. "That's what the

announcer for the White Sox said every time a Sox player hit a homerun."

"Do you want me to call Ray and Anna and divert them to this location?"

Mack took his time to think. There were still unanswered questions and too many unknowns. "No, let them finish their job at the port. It's more likely Paddy is being held there."

"While we wait for them to get in position, I'll send you everything I have on Tiger Products and the property on Kribensis Manor. A word of caution. It will take me time to get a nighttime drone up. Unfortunately, they are all in use so I may have trouble commandeering one."

"I appreciate whatever you can get me, Nims. Call me when you know more."

Mack slid the phone into his pocket and headed across the room to Gray and Malloy. As he neared, he heard Gray explaining to Malloy the letter of intent granting the recharging station rights to LeBeau and his investor, Total Energy.

"Sorry to interrupt," Mack said. "Mind if I use your computer for a few minutes, Steve?"

"Let me print out this Letter of Intent and then it's

all yours." Gray tapped a couple keys then pushed the computer over to Mack.

Mack slid the computer down a few chairs. He turned the laptop so that Malloy and Gray couldn't see the screen. He opened Google Maps and typed in Kribensis Manor. A satellite view of the area showed a sparsely populated development with a number of new construction sites. Mack wondered how current the photograph was.

Mack swiveled his chair to face Malloy and Gray. Gray stopped talking when he noticed Mack facing him.

"Pius," Mack said, "do you know a housing development on the outskirts of Dublin called Kribensis Manor?"

Malloy looked up at the ceiling in thought then brought his eyes down to Mack. "Yes, Kribensis Manor is northwest of the city, why?"

"What kind of development is it?"

"The concept was to create a very posh, very exclusive community. The houses were designed to be near-mansions, like the exclusive communities in America."

"What can you tell me about the development?"

"Not much, I've only been there once to visit Claire and Finn Donovan. At that time, there were only two houses completed."

"Paddy's sister?"

"She and her husband developed Kribensis Manor. They live in one of the completed houses, why?"

"Nothing in particular, just my curiosity for real estate. I remember asking Paddy if I bought a place in Dublin, where would he recommend. When you said Kribensis Manor it came back to me."

"You might get a good deal if you want to buy. The development didn't turn out as expected and the prices have tanked."

"If I wanted to go take a look at a place there, what's the best way to get there?"

"It's very easy. From here take Old Cabra Road, which runs into Navan Road. Follow that to the M3. Once you get on the highway, get off on the first exit. Then follow the signs to Kribensis Manor."

"I might just do that after we finish up the deal."

Mack studied the satellite to get a feel of the development. The two finished houses were at opposite ends of the development. The remaining land was a grid of what looked like unfinished construction sites or empty lots.

He debated whether to ask Malloy which house Claire Donovan lived in. Since there were only two completed houses, he had a fifty-fifty chance of picking the right house.

Mack brought Gray's laptop back to him. "Thanks Steve, can we talk for a second?" Mack walked away and stopped after ten steps.

Gray stood and stretched then strolled over to Mack. "What do you need?"

Mack handed O'May's phone to Gray. "Keep this with you and if Nimesh calls while I'm away, do whatever he asks. If Ray or Anna call, tell them I'll be back shortly."

Gray looked quizzically at Mack. "Where are you going?"

Mack thought about telling Gray his plan then realized the less Gray knew the less he'd have to lie.

"I want to take Pogladek's temperature so we can finally put this deal to bed. I shouldn't be gone long."

§

CHAPTER 26

Mack left the conference room with a measured pace. He had the satellite photo of Kribensis Manor burned in his mind and knew he had to come up with a plan to rescue Paddy - if he was there.

At the top of the stairs, he paused. Before a plan could be sussed out, he needed to get the lay of the land, know what he was up against.

As he slowly descended the stairs he realized the first step was to figure out how best to get to Kribensis Manor without being seen. From there, he'd determine which house to check out first.

Approaching the front entrance, he decided a taxi would be easiest and fastest. The taxi could drop him off a quarter mile away and he'd hoof it the rest of the way.

He reached into his pocket to call a taxi and realized he no longer had a phone but had plenty of cash. He'd have to hail a cab and prayed one would be along soon.

He pushed through the door and strolled out to the sidewalk. He looked right to see an empty road. He looked left to see no movement on the road. The only vehicle in sight was hundred yards down. It was a white van parked on the wrong side of the road.

"Damn," Mack said when he saw the white van. Before he could react he felt a jab in his lower back.

"Keep your eyes forward," a woman's voice said. "Stay calm and you won't get hurt. If you don't follow my orders, I'll pull the trigger and sever your spinal cord. You'll be alive but all your bodily functions below where the bullet enters will no longer work."

She had a tinge of exhilaration in her voice.

"What do you want?" Mack asked trying not to show fear.

"I just told you, Mr. Mack. If you don't do as I say, you'll never walk again and Paddy O'May will be dead. I get paid either way." She sounded almost giddy.

"Is this about the money?"

"Of course. Everything is about money."

The van pulled up and the side door slid open. A skinny man with a ski mask over his face grabbed Mack by the front of his shirt and pulled him inside. He shoved him down and kicked Mack's feet together.

Mack grimaced from the pain shooting out of his ribs. The skinny man smiled and wagged his tongue outside his ski mask as if he was enjoying himself. He reached down and wrapped a rope around Mack's ankles and tied a knot.

Mack looked away anticipating another kick.

"Turn around, lie on your stomach and put your hands behind your back," the woman said as she climbed in and slid the door shut.

Mack's hands were tied tightly together. The woman slipped a black hood over his head.

The van drove away quickly.

Lying on his stomach, Mack felt pain with every bump in the road and the few turns they made. When he felt the van turn right and leave the smooth pavement, its pace began to slow. The short ride was bumpy and slow with little turns like the van was driving through an obstacle course.

The van stopped and both front doors opened.

"Untie his feet," the woman ordered as the side door opened.

As soon as the rope around his ankles was removed, the woman said, "Bring him around to the driver's side."

The skinny man dragged Mack by his right foot across the van floor. He sat Mack up and told him to step out of the van.

Mack felt the ground below his feet. It felt like packed dirt.

The skinny man seized Mack by the arm, jerked him to the right and pulled him forward. Mack stumbled and the man squeezed his grip to hold him up. After two right turns, the man said, "Stop and don't move."

The skinny man walked back around the van. With the hood over his head, Mack's hearing became acute.

On the other side of the van, Mack heard the skinny man plead, "I won't say anything, I promise."

What sounded like a soft gunshot was followed by a high-pitched whimper and strange thump. He heard a commotion and then the van door slid closed. Mack knew what just happened.

Footsteps grew louder and he sensed someone coming toward him. He inhaled deeply and braced, thinking he was next.

"Relax, you're not done. Turn around and keep your mouth shut."

Mack slowly turned around. His steps were uncertain, testing the ground as he turned. When he stopped, the woman pulled the hood off his head.

"You see that house straight ahead of you?"

Mack nodded and felt the barrel of a gun pressed against his lower back. The same spot as before.

"Walk to the door at a leisurely pace."

Mack started walking and asked, "Did you just kill that man?"

The woman laughed easily — like Mack just asked a stupid question.

"Why?"

"He saw my face."

Her answer unnerved Mack. They walked in silence until they reached the steps leading up to a long, narrow front porch.

She untied Mack's hands and said, "Knock hard once, wait three seconds and knock twice."

Mack did as ordered and heard footsteps inside the house coming to the door.

"Who is it?" A woman's voice came through the door.

"Special delivery," the woman behind Mack said forcefully.

The door opened and standing in the doorway was Paddy O'May's sister, Claire Donovan. She held the door handle with her left hand. A tall man dressed like he was heading to the polo club stood behind her. He had a vacant gaze and an affected grin on his face.

Claire Donovan smirked, stepped back and swept her right arm behind her gesturing for them to enter.

The woman shoved Mack inside and followed him in.

"Thank you Becca," Donovan said.

Mack wondered if Becca would shoot Claire and the

man standing behind her because they had definitely seen her face.

"Where's J Otis?" Becca asked.

"Upstairs in his room with one of the girls. He's not to be disturbed."

"What am I to do with Mr. Mack?"

"Put him down in the cellar," Claire Donovan said.

"You think that's a good idea?"

"No, but we're improvising since our original plan fell apart. Do you have a better idea?"

"Yes, shoot him and dispose of the body."

Mack felt Becca run the barrel of the pistol across the nape of this neck.

"Not until we get our money. That part of the plan has never changed." Claire Donovan pushed the door closed. "After that, he's all yours."

Becca stuck the barrel against the back of Mack's head. She said, "Finn, take him downstairs and make sure the door is securely locked before you come back up."

Finn grabbed Mack by the back of the neck and led

him away.

As they walked away, Becca said, "After you secure him in the cellar go upstairs and tell J Otis to get dressed and get his ass down here."

A look of dread spread over Finn's face.

Finn tightened his grip on Mack's neck as they descended into the cellar. At the bottom of the steps they came to a metal door with a turning wheel in the center. It was a door found on sea going ships.

"Open the door," Finn ordered.

Mack loosened the latches, turned the wheel and the door popped open.

Finn shoved Mack into the room. The door closed with a clang, which echoed through the cellar. The sparsely furnished room had two cheap lamps in opposite corners and two wooden chairs halfway between the lamps. One lamp was dimly lit.

Paddy O'May sat on the cement floor in the corner with his knees pulled up to his chest and his head resting on his arms.

§

CHAPTER 27

Without looking up, Paddy O'May raised his hands as if to protect himself and said, "Please don't..."

Seeing O'May's reaction sent a shiver through Mack. He squatted on his haunches next to O'May and couldn't help but look him over. O'May had a black eye and bruised chin from an obviously brutal beating. His right hand was purple and swollen around the knuckles.

"Paddy, it's Billy," Mack said and waited for O'May to lift his head.

A look of despair on O'May's face turned to joy. It only lasted a second when O'May looked around and realized where he was. He slowly closed his eyes and lowered his chin in defeat.

"Don't give up Paddy," Mack said a little too cheerfully. "To quote the greatest baseball philosopher, 'It ain't over till it's over.'"

O'May tried to muster a smile but failed.

Mack stood and walked around the dimly lit room. The floor was cement and the walls were cinderblock. There were two windows high up on one wall. A toilet with a shower curtain hanging around it stood in the opposite corner.

Mack checked the door and it was sealed tight. He strolled back over by O'May, grabbed one of the wooden chairs and brought it below one of the windows. He stepped up and tried to open it. The window was sealed shut and wouldn't budge.

"I already checked the windows," O'May said. "They are firmly sealed shut."

Mack closely examined the clear gel between the window and the frame. Outside, a man walked past the window and kept going. Mack brought his left arm up and checked his watch. He stood silently on the chair with one eye on the window and the other on his wristwatch.

The man walked by the window again. Mack checked

the time: one minute, twenty-two seconds.

Mack waited for the man to walk past again. He checked his watch: one minute twenty-seven seconds.

He stepped off the chair and carried it over to O'May. He motioned for O'May to stand then went over and brought the other chair to O'May. He said, "Sit on the chair and let's talk."

"I'm fine where I am, Billy."

"I need you to sit on the chair and help me time the guard walking the past the window. We can figure out what we can do, if anything, while we time him."

O'May sat on the chair and looked skeptically at Mack.

"I know it looks bleak, but if we act defeated, we are defeated." Mack sensed O'May didn't buy his words. "Tell me what happened from the beginning. That may spur something in you or me."

"It's hopeless, Billy."

"Humor me."

"Fine." O'May massaged his temples in circles like he was rewinding his memory. "After we spoke outside the conference room, I decided to head back to the workshop and keep busy until the dinner. I stopped in the bathroom and before I know it, two guys grabbed me and threw me against the wall." O'May rubbed the back of his head then continued, "I banged my head against the wall pretty hard but didn't black out. The two men jumped me, we scuffled but they were too much for me. They taped my mouth shut and my hands behind my back. One of the men cleared the hall before they rushed me outside and into a car with blacked out windows. In the car, a hood was put over my head and I was ordered to lie down. The next thing I knew I was in an old factory. A bit later, some woman shows up and shoots one of the men. Then she brought me here."

"Did you get a good look at the two guys and the woman?"

O'May nodded. "The two guys were the American tax officials that came to the workshop earlier."

"How about the woman?"

"I only saw the side of her face but when she executed one of those guys, I didn't dare look at her."

"What else can you tell me?"

"Why? It's hopeless. There's no way out."

O'May was throwing in the towel and Mack knew if

they had any chance of getting out of the cellar, he had to get O'May's mind occupied on something positive.

"Tell me again how you came up with the breakthrough technology for your magnet engine. I never tire of hearing it."

The corner of O'May's mouth flicked up and a spark of life came back to his eyes.

"As you know, I wanted to create a friction free engine using the vector field of magnets. Magnetic fields both attract and repel. I thought I could replicate the pistons in a combustion engine and eliminate the friction of metal on metal by using electromagnets and harnessing electric currents to attract and repel the magnets. I needed a new way to secure the moving parts. Metal was out of the question so I tried industrial epoxies to act like nuts and bolts, depending on the viscosity, this idea had promise as a catalyst."

"Keep it simple, like you're explaining it to a six grader," Mack said.

"After a bunch of failed experiments, I stumbled onto a combination of epoxies that if used for different reasons not only eliminated all friction, but when used together, recycled the electricity used to drive the magnets back and forth, like a piston. One epoxy cures at a very high temperature and is used to coat the electromagnets. Through trial and error, I learned if copper wire, coated in a different epoxy, is run along the electromagnet, this connection excites the electrons and the copper wire conducts and channels the electricity into a current driving the magnets. Simply put, this should not have happened. The reaction should have been the opposite. In any case, I ran that electric current back to the battery, recharging it at a slightly slower rate than the engine was using."

"So the epoxies are key to the technology?"

O'May nodded. "There are different epoxies and different reactions to heat and electrical charges. The viscosity of most industrial epoxies requires very high temperatures or high voltage currents before a reaction occurs. Most household epoxies react at lower temperatures and normal household currents."

"What do you mean by react?"

"Some harden, some soften."

Mack looked up at the window. The man walked by again: One minute, twenty-five seconds.

"These windows are sealed shut by some kind of glue or epoxy, right? If we heat up the window, what would likely happen?"

O'May sat up, excited then slumped back down. "We don't have what we need to heat it up to a needed temperature."

Mack eyed the dimly lit lamp. "What about an electrical current?"

O'May walked over to the window and looked up, inspecting the gap between the window and the frame.

Mack carried over a wooden chair and placed it next to O'May. "This'll help you get a closer look."

O'May stood on the chair and closely examined the gap. He used his finger to feel the clear gel filling the gap. "If it's a household epoxy, like superglue, an electric current might breakdown the viscosity." O'May ran his finger along the gap and said, "I don't know how we do it."

Mack marched over to the unlit lamp in the corner. He pushed the lamp over, gripped the cord and yanked twice. He pulled out the cord and examined the end. Enough wire was exposed to jam into the gel filling the gap.

Mack plugged the cord into the electrical socket and stood on the chair so the gap was eye level.

O'May jerked the plug from the outlet and shook his head. "Insert the wires in the gel before you plug in. The metal will be highly electrified once the current is running through the wire."

Mack's face grew dark pink. "Thanks," he said without looking at O'May. He jammed the wires into the gel.

"Step away," O'May said. "This will take a little time."

"What do we do now?"

O'May shrugged and said, "We wait a few minutes then test it. Before we test the window, we unplug."

Mack said, "Before we test, we take into consideration the guard patrolling outside. We time everything based on him."

As soon as the guard walked past, Mack stepped up on the chair and gestured for O'May to unplug. The window remained sealed shut. He gestured for O'May to plug back in and stepped down off the chair.

They did this two more times with the same result. On the third try the window jiggled. It was beginning to loosen.

"We should wait for two passes by the guard for our

next try," O'May said.

After the second pass, Mack pushed on the window and it opened. With his finger, he scraped away the gel and closed the window.

He said, "Bring that chair over here next to me. On the next pass, we go."

After the guard walked by, Mack waited ten seconds before he steadily slid open the window. He boosted O'May through the window and whispered, "Climb over the wall straight ahead and wait for me, staying out of sight."

He watched O'May run across the opening, jump up and pull himself up and over the wall. He closed the window and waited for the guard.

The guard passed and he waited ten seconds, slid the window open and crawled through. He closed the window and sprinted across the opening. He hit the wall running, grabbed the top and flung himself over it in one motion.

He crouched on his haunches to see O'May on his knees with his hands on top of his head. Two men stood a few feet away with pistols pointed. One man held a flashlight.

"Put your hands on your head, like your friend here."

§

CHAPTER 28

The narrow, intense beam from the flashlight blinded Mack. He turned his head away and looked over at O'May. The little man's head was down and he nervously twitched his arms.

The beam from the flashlight scanned Mack's body. He assumed the once-over was a check for weapons. When the beam returned to his face, He looked straight into the light.

"Mr. Mack?" the voice from behind the flashlight said close to a whisper.

Mack nodded and checked on O'May again.

The beam of light left Mack and now shined up on the face of the man holding it.

Mack's eyes widened as if he's seen a ghost.

The man laughed easily then said, "No, you're not seeing a ghost."

Mack tried to speak but only guttural sounds came out. When he collected himself, he said, "Officer McNee? You were shot and killed?"

"Shot yes, killed no." He tapped his chest with the butt end of the flashlight. "Thank God for bulletproof vests." He pointed to his left. "And for this guy here." The beam of light hit the emaciated face."

"Nigel?"

"He found me and called it in."

Mack slowly returned his gaze to McNee. "I didn't think anything could stop a bullet at that range," he said, thankful the man who saved his life was alive and standing in front of him.

"I broke a rib and have a deep multicolored bruise across my chest." McNee shined the beam at a point on the ground and said, "We can talk about what happened later. Both of you need to come with me." He pointed the beam away from the brick wall and at a half-built house.

McNee led Mack and O'May across a large patch of

dirt and into the semi finished house. Waters followed at a distance.

The walls were rough cinderblocks and the floor was gray cement. Wooden beams high above ran between the walls. There were large square openings where the windows would eventually be and no roof.

They silently walked through the exposed house. At the front end of the house a group of six people stood in a circle, staring at a tablet screen. A small lantern on the ground in the center of the circle dimly illuminated the area. Mack recognized Detective Dillon who held the tablet out for everyone to see while she pointed at a spot on the screen and spoke in a hushed tone.

"Boss," Officer McNee said, "look who I found." He shined the beam of light on Mack's face then slid it over and down to O'May who squeezed his eyes shut when the beam hit his face.

Dillon didn't speak at first. She looked over at Mack. She kept her eyes on him as she handed the tablet to the officer on her right.

She walked over and looked him up and down as if she didn't believe it. Mack tried to read her expression but came up with a blank.

She turned, did the same thing to O'May then motioned with her fingers for McNee to join them.

She smiled ever so slightly and said, "Okay Timmy, fill me in."

McNee gestured to Mack for him to answer.

Mack started to retell their escape then abruptly stopped. He realized he was so relieved to be out of the basement that it didn't dawn on him that Dillon and her team were there and not at the port as planned.

He blinked repeatedly and asked, "How did you know Paddy and I were here?"

"The raid on the hotel at the docks was successful. We found a dozen teenage girls ready to be moved. The raid was quick but when we didn't find Paddy there, I called his phone to speak with you. You weren't there so Ray Gunn called Nimesh and he figured you were coming here. We commandeered a helicopter and landed a quarter mile down the road so we could stop you from doing something stupid." She looked at Mack with a smirk. "I'm not surprised you were caught trying to be the hero."

"That's not what happened." From the look on Dillon's face, Mack realized she didn't believe him.

Mack filled her in on his abduction on the street outside the conference room building, being brought to the basement prison cell and how O'May was able to run an electric charge into the window, loosening the window and allowing them to make their escape. He made sure to stress the presence of a guard patrolling outside the house.

When Mack finished, Dillon said, "Something doesn't make sense." She waved for the man holding the tablet to come over. "Jasko, bring the tablet over please?"

She turned the screen of the tablet to face Mack. What looked like a technicolor X-ray filled on the screen. The image was mainly black and dark green with sporadic glowing yellow dots. Human figures in deep orange were also on the screen. From the angle, there were figures on both the upper floor and the ground floor. Some figures were moving, some were sitting and some were lying down.

Dillon pointed at two figures in the lower right corner, both in a sitting position.

"We were under the working assumption those two figures were you and Mr. O'May."

"We were in the basement," Mack said.

"This technology is great but doesn't work well below ground. Besides, the plans for this house registered with the Housing Agency do not include a basement."

Mack counted the people on the screen. Three figures were upstairs in a room and five were on the ground level. Except for the two sitting in the right corner of the screen, the three others in the middle of the house were standing near each other. Mack guessed they were in conversation.

"Can you identify any of these people?" Mack asked.

Dillon shook her head. "Not definitively, but since the house belongs to Claire and Finn Donovan, they're probably inside."

"My sister?" O'May said loudly.

"Shhhh," Dillon hissed. "We don't know why they are here. They could be involved or could be hostages. We just don't know. Ray and Anna are reconnoitering the house and the situation. We'll know more when they get back."

"There's one way to find out," O'May said as he started walking toward the house to confront his sister.

"Get back here," Dillon ordered.

Mack hurried over, grabbed O'May by the shoulders and turned him around.

Dillon said, "We have a trail of dead bodies, a dozen teenage girls who were about to disappear into the sex trade, many of them already strung out, and you want to take matters into your own hands?"

O'May struggled to free himself from Mack's grasp.

"There are likely two young girls in that house that belong back with their families. So, sit down and shut up or I'll have you dragged away in chains."

Mack added, "Paddy, if she is involved, you can do what you have to do after this is over."

He gently maneuvered O'May back to the group and relaxed his grip but didn't let go.

Mack and O'May froze when the sound of footsteps approached. Dillon and each officer drew their pistols and pointed toward the sound.

Out of the darkness a voice said, "Stand down, it's Ray Gunn."

Gunn came around the corner of the cinder block wall, grimacing as he approached the group. Anna Swerdlov stayed two steps behind him, studying the screen on her phone.

When he saw Mack, Gunn stopped in his tracks. Swerdlov nearly bumped into him.

Swerdlov looked up from her phone and looked at Mack. She marched over looking at him as if he were about to get scolded and spanked. She stood close and said, "You disobeyed my orders and, more importantly, my good advice." She threw her arms around him and hugged him tight. She whispered in his ear, "You could have been killed." She let go, stepped back and slapped him just hard enough to sting.

"We have a headcount," Gunn said. "Inside the house are Clair and Finn Donovan, Becca, J Otis and two young girls, one of which is Anna's little sister. We don't know who the other one is."

"I do," Nigel Waters said. "It's my daughter."

"Who are the other two?" Mack asked.

Before Gunn answered, he looked over at O'May and held his gaze. "Kieran Sweeney and Pius Malloy."

§

CHAPTER 29

"How did Malloy and Sweeney end up here?" Mack asked.

"When Gray went to fax the letter to LeBeau he returned to an empty conference room. He figured they left to get some air or something."

Dillon waved her hand. "Shhh, Something's up," she said. "The people in the house are moving around frantically, like they're running in circles."

Dillon brought the tablet over to Mack, Gunn and Swerdlov. "Any idea why?"

"They just realized Paddy and I escaped," Mack said. He smiled triumphantly.

"Settle down Billy, the game isn't over yet," Swerdlov

said sternly. "My sister is still inside."

Ray Gunn ran his hand over his baldhead in thought. "We don't know for sure why there is unusual movement inside." He pulled his phone from his back pocket, punched in a number and held the phone out for everyone to hear.

"Nimesh," he said, "is it possible to get the drone closer without alerting those inside the house?"

"It's not the people inside the house we have to worry about, it's the guard patrolling the perimeter."

"Good to know. We'll incapacitate the guard first. When that's done, move the clone as close as possible so we have a sharper image of the hostiles inside as we clear the building."

"Copy that, but the images are heat sensors so they can only get so refined."

"Will we be able to distinguish between say a girl and grown woman?"

"Easily."

"Gather around," Gunn said, "From my experience, we don't have much time before something bad happens."

Swerdlov nodded in agreement as she walked to Gunn.

"Our objective is to clear the house with nobody getting hurt," Gunn said firmly. He looked at Swerdlov expecting her to add something. She got the message.

"Once the guard is taken out, that leaves the back door exposed. We create a diversion at the front of the house and I slip in through the back. I will -"

"Billy Mack," a voice called out into the night air. "Billy Mack, we have to talk."

All eyes shifted to Mack. He shrugged to indicate he was as surprised as anyone.

Dillon raised her hand to get her officer's attention. When all the officers were focused on her, she said, "Go."

The officers scattered, each headed to a specific location. McNee remained behind and stood next to Dillon. She looked around and said, "We prepared for a shooter situation and will have the house covered from every angle."

"The orders are to only engage the shooter, right?" Swerdlov asked. "My little sister is inside."

"As is my daughter," Waters added.

Dillon ignored the question. She walked over to Mack with McNee step for step beside her.

"Billy Mack," the voice called out again. "You have one minute to show yourself or I start shooting."

Mack didn't like the feeling in his gut. The voice had to be Becca and she had no reservation, no conscience when shooting someone. Was she calling him out to kill him?

"You don't have to do this, Billy," Swerdlov said. "We can do this our way."

Mack shook his head. "I gotta do what I gotta do."

Mack looked over to Gunn to see if he had anything to say. Gunn's back was to him as he conversed quietly with Dillon and McNee. He turned to face Mack.

"Officer McNee will go with you."

"Why give her another target?" Mack asked.

"She's not stupid. She won't shoot a cop unless she's cornered."

McNee walked over to Mack, stuck out his hand and said, "Let's do this, Mr. Mack."

Shaking McNee's hand strangely comforted Mack.

"It's Billy," he said.

"I'm Timmy. Stay close to me so we can talk quietly. Never get in front of me. We'll have to improvise as we get a handle on the situation. Most importantly, I'm armed and vested so if she points a weapon at you, slide behind me if you can."

Mack and McNee walked around the corner of the cinderblock wall and across a large patch of dirt to the driveway of the Donovan house. Mack eyed two silver Mercedes parked on the side of the house. If someone was inside one or both of the cars, they could easily run over him and McNee. Luckily, the engines weren't running.

On the front porch, standing at the top of the steps was Becca with her arm around the neck of Pius Malloy and her gun stuck in his temple. The porch light behind Becca shined bright, making it difficult to make out their faces.

"No cops," Becca said. "Tell your boyfriend to get lost."

"Not happening," McNee said. He smiled to see her reaction.

She pointed the pistol at Mack.

Mack moved shoulder to shoulder with McNee, not behind him like McNee had ordered.

Becca brought the pistol back to Malloy's temple. "I don't give a damn who I shoot first, this guy or the tall skinny guy inside."

Mack had no doubt she would gladly shoot Malloy and then Sweeney. He looked at Malloy trembling with Becca's arm around his neck. Malloy was pleading with eyes for Mack to do what she said.

Mack tilted his head toward McNee and said, "I've seen her kill in cold blood. She enjoys it. Let me do this."

"Bad idea."

"Timmy, J Otis Weil is inside the house. If he wants me dead, he'll want to gloat over me first. I can buy enough time for Anna to get into the house."

McNee didn't answer right away. He kept his stare on Becca.

"I still think it's a bad idea." He sniffed then added, "Stall as much as you can. Walk slowly and keep your antennae up."

Walking slowly would not be a problem, Mack thought. Walking toward a gun held by someone who enjoys killing does not speed you up.

"Alright, I'm backing off," McNee said loudly. "If anyone dies inside that house, I'll be the last person you see in this world."

"This isn't Hollywood," Becca said but her voice wasn't menacing, it had a hint of hesitation.

McNee stepped backward until he reached the end of the driveway. He disappeared behind the wall.

Mack's first step was tentative. He steeled himself and started toward the porch, slowly. It wasn't an act.

At the bottom of the steps Mack stopped and looked at Malloy and then Becca.

She stepped back, pulling Malloy with her. The pistol never left his temple.

"Come up here and kneel down in front of me," Becca ordered.

When Mack dropped to his knees, she released Malloy and said, "Get your ass back inside."

"Let him go," Mack said. "He's done nothing to deserve this."

"Stand up," Becca said as flicked the pistol up and

down. She took another step back.

Mack stood, never taking his eyes off hers.

She moved behind Mack and jammed the pistol into his lower spine. "You do anything stupid and I'll paralyze you before I kill you." She nudged Mack forward with the barrel of the pistol. "Inside until I tell you to stop."

As Mack walked across the hardwood floor, the room was empty. He tried to determine how anyone would get inside. At the far end of the room was a large sectional sofa and two wingback chairs, one near each end of the sofa. There was blood on the wingback chair left of the sofa. He walked toward the sofa until Becca said, "Stop."

Mack stopped and continued to take in the room without moving his head. A small opening at eleven o'clock led into the kitchen. He eyed a silver refrigerator against the wall. Further left was a set of stairs to the second level. They were carpeted and the railing was black iron. The curtains were closed covering every window. There was no one else in the room.

Mack wondered where the figures he'd seen on the tablet had gone. It was only he and Becca in the room. He prayed Gunn, Swerdlov and Dillon were watching on the tablet.

Mack heard footsteps coming down the stairs. He turned to see J Otis with a wicked smile on his face. He wore gray pants, a blue shirt with no tie and a blue blazer. On his feet were topsiders and no socks as if dressed for a night on a boat.

Two beautiful teenage girls walked tentatively behind him. Mack studied the taller girl, a thin blonde with her hair pulled back in a ponytail. She wore a loose black tank top and white gym shorts. Her makeup couldn't hide her frightened eyes. The other girl was a shapely brunette with her hair in pigtails. She wore a white tank top with black gym shorts and little, if any makeup. From the look in her eyes, Mack knew she was high.

"Billy Mack," J Otis said, "I know what you're thinking, I always do. You're thinking how the fuck did I let J Otis get the upper hand." J Otis pulled the brunette to him and kissed her hard, like he was the victor. He pushed her away and grinned at Mack. The girl smiled meekly.

J Otis walked over to Becca. "Give me your gun," he said and held out his hand.

Becca chuckled. "Get your own gun."

J Otis acted like the rebuke was nothing but Mack could sense he was seething inside. J Otis was pathological and could manipulate his expressions.

"Here's what's going to happen," J Otis said, his voice now different, his tone matter of fact. "If you want to live, you will call that blonde bimbo you're with and have her bring Paddy O'May to me. She has until eight this morning to deliver him. If he's not here by then, Malloy and Sweeney are dead."

J Otis turned to Becca and said, "Go get Claire and Finn."

"And leave you alone with him? He'll break you in two as soon as I'm gone. You go get them."

J Otis stomped over the stairs and took them two at a time.

Out of the corner of his eye, Mack thought he saw someone zip across the kitchen. He needed to distract Becca.

Before he came up with a way to distract her, J Otis came bounding down the steps followed by Claire and Finn Donovan. Finn carried a heavy duffle bag in his left hand.

"Stay here," he said and strolled over to Mack. "Once Paddy O'May is here, you will go to the bank and transfer the funds to the account you were given. As soon as we confirm receipt of the ten million, O'May will be released."

Mack looked over at Claire Donovan. He waited until she looked at him then said, "He's not going to let your brother go. He's in bed with the Russian President, meaning the Russian mafia. The Russians can't allow your brother's brilliant invention to succeed. It will virtually eliminate the oil and gas industry, the only money keeping the country from becoming third world. As soon as the money hits your account, he's dead."

Claire shook her head in disbelief. "Why should I listen to you? You've taken advantage of Paddy since the first minute you met him. He should own a hundred percent of his own company."

Mack stifled a laugh at her absurd logic. "When J Otis is done, your brother will be dead and there will be no company."

"J Otis gave me his word and I trust him. He's already paid us half up front in cash." She pointed to the duffel bag in Finn's hand.

A gunshot rang out and Finn Donovan fell to the floor screaming in pain. He let go the duffel bag and grabbed his left thigh as blood soaked through his pant leg.

J Otis sprinted toward the front door. Another shot rang out. J Otis stumbled as he headed to the door. He grabbed his right shoulder but never stopped running. Another shot rang out hitting the doorframe above his head. It didn't slow him down.

Mack felt Becca's arm around his neck and the barrel of her pistol against his temple. She slowly backed away pulling Mack with her. They were headed to the kitchen.

A gunshot from outside echoed through the house. Mack heard J Otis yell, "Goddamnit."

Anna Swerdlov stood at the base of the steps, her gun still pointing at the front doorway.

Claire Donovan screeched and rushed Swerdlov, tackling her before Swerdlov reacted. Donovan rolled on top of Swerdlov as she tried to wrestle away the gun.

The last thing Mack saw before Becca pulled him into the kitchen was Waters rushing through the front door with his pistol in front of him.

"Even the slightest sound and it's over for you," Becca said.

Mack nodded just enough to let her know he understood. The sound of a car starting and the engine revving reverberated through the kitchen.

Mack heard a scream coming from the other room and then a thud as if something big and soft was dropped on the hardwood floor.

Becca suddenly stopped pulling and Mack was sure it was all over. She was going to shoot him and make a run for the car. The barrel of the pistol pulled away from his temple and her grip eased.

"Drop your weapon and let go of Billy," Ray Gunn said so forcefully that Mack eased his fingers as if he were dropping the gun.

When the clang of her gun hit the tile floor, Mack spun around. Ray Gunn had a handful of Becca's hair and his Smith & Wesson stuck in the back of her head.

Becca smiled easily at Mack and said, "You win some you lose some."

Waters stood in the opening to the kitchen hugging his daughter so tight Mack thought he would break.

Swerdlov walked into the room with her arm tightly around her little sister. "The Donovans are in need of an ambulance."

She pointed her gun at Becca. "She's mine."

§

EPILOGUE

A week later, Mack sat in the boardroom of The Celtic Horse's new offices across the street from the factory. The sound of industrial motors, heavy cranes and an occasional jackhammer coming from across the street provided the background music. Ray Gunn, Paddy O'May and Kieran Sweeney sat around the table, each with a cup of coffee in front of them.

Paddy O'May's bruises were healing nicely but the scar of his sister betraying him would never heal. From their hospital beds, she and her husband, Finn pleaded guilty to perjury, bribery, money laundering and multiple fraud charges including bank fraud and wire fraud. Aiding and abetting in the kidnapping of O'May was still hanging over them but Paddy was reluctant to work with the police on these charges. Mack was surprised Paddy was so forgiving especially after his sister repeatedly called him demanding, no screaming she be given ownership in the company. Paddy's reluctance to help authorities didn't matter. There was enough in the financial crimes to send them both away for a couple of lifetimes.

Mack looked at his watch and said, "Where's Pius? I don't want to start without him."

As if on cue, Malloy strolled into the boardroom with a stack of papers in his right hand. He stopped and held up the papers. "These are orders and deposits for over a hundred thousand engines and that's just with the European carmakers. The Americans and Asian orders should be in this week."

Everyone except Billy Mack clapped vigorously.

As soon as the clapping subsided, Mack asked, "When do the carmakers expect delivery?"

Malloy placed the papers on the table and sat. "It's going to take at least six months for each carmaker to retool their factories In my office is a schedule Kieran and I have been working on with each carmaker. If our factory is up and running in two months, we will easily meet demand."

"The engine is not complicated to build," O'May

said. "With three shifts on the line, we can produce fifty thousand a month, give or take. The charging stations are more complicated but we will run parallel manufacturing. Plus, we don't need as many of the charging units."

For the next thirty minutes the group discussed the operations of the company and what targets were to be met for internal operations and for investors.

When the meeting ended, Ray Gunn stood and said, "We will leave you to run your business." He put his hands on the table and leaned down. "One last point. The security I hired is in place. For the time being, there will be two guards at each door, a team for both in the factory and in the office. Your homes will have twenty-four hour security. For the time being, you will be driven to and from work." Gunn saw the concern on everyone's faces. "This is not negotiable. For the near future, everyone at the company is a potential target. On the plus side, there will be a monthly security review and once the engine is on the market, security will be reduced to normal corporate security." Gunn pointed at The Celtic Horse management team. "The three of you will soon be billionaires and will require a certain level of personal security. A man named Nimesh will be here next week to instruct you on what to look for, what security you need, shit like that. Welcome to your new world."

Gunn shook hands with Sweeney and Malloy. He gripped O'May by the shoulders, leaned in and whispered in his ear. "You're a tough nut, keep it up. The speech you gave at the closing dinner in front of that crowd was inspiring. It's an honor to know you." He spun on his heel and marched out the room.

Mack took that as his signal to leave. "I'll see you all for breakfast tomorrow."

By the time Mack reached the street, Gunn sat in the backseat of an idling taxi. Mack climbed in and pulled the door closed.

"Fitzwilliam Hotel," Gunn said to the driver.

After the taxi pulled out onto Ballymun Road, Mack asked, "Why are we going to the Fitzwilliam Hotel?"

"We're having lunch at Glovers Alley... your treat."

"Let me call my credit card and up my limit," Mack replied.

"Put it on your company card, it has no limit."

Mack looked over at Gunn to make sure he was

serious.

"You're a partner now Billy, if it's not a valid business expense, accounting takes it out of your pay."

When the taxi stopped in front of the Fitzwilliam, Gunn said to Mack, "Pay the man and meet me inside."

Mack dug into his pocket, pulled out a fifty Euro note and gave it to the driver. "Keep the change."

"Thank you sir," the driver said staring happily at the orange and white note in his hand totaling twice the fare.

Mack strolled into the hotel lobby to see Gunn disappear down a hall. He turned right and headed in that direction. The short hallway ended at a dark wooden door. Mack turned the handle and pushed open the door.

Sitting around an elegantly set table was Anna Swerdlov, Bridget Dillon, Timmy McNee and Nigel Waters. Ray Gunn stood off in the corner next to a waiter pouring wine into a glass for Gunn to taste.

"Thank you. I'm sure it's fine. Fill everyone's glass," Gunn said as he walked over to the table.

Mack sat next to Waters. He looked around the table, perplexed. Two people were missing.

Swerdlov sensed Mack's confusion. "My sister is visiting Nigel's daughter, Fiona in Belfast today."

Mack looked over at Waters, still confused.

Waters patted Mack's arm. "Fiona is in a drug rehab facility. J Otis Weil got her hooked on drugs as soon as he had her." Waters tried to grin. "The therapist is optimistic she'll be out in a month to six weeks. She's tough but the added the shock of her mother's death makes it all still raw."

Mack glanced over to Swerdlov.

"My sister is doing fine, considering. My aunt and cousin from Russia are over and helping."

Gunn sat and raised his glass. "To Alexa and Fiona."

Everyone raised their glass, nodded and took a sip of their wine.

Silence hung over the table for a few minutes.

Finally, Mack said, "I know this is of secondary importance but The Celtic Horse is on track thanks to you."

"Do each of us get a free car?" McNee asked.

Mack smiled and changed the subject. "Detective

Dillon, what are your plans now?"

"Call me Bridget, please." She took a sip of wine and said, "I will be co-heading a new Europe-wide sex trafficking enforcement unit. Timmy here is my right hand."

McNee grinned proudly. "About the free car?" he asked.

"Who is the other co-head?" Mack asked, ignoring McNee.

"I am," Swerdlov said. "I will be heading the intelligence unit. My first target is J Otis Weil. When we take him down it will put the fear of God in every other trafficker and pimp."

Mack didn't doubt she would succeed but said, "It won't be easy."

"We're already inside his organization."

Mack sat back. "So quick?"

"We turned Becca. She's our eyes and ears on the inside."

"Can you trust her?"

Mack saw Ray Gunn smiling. He had a hand in

turning Becca.

"She was a victim herself. As a teenager, her stepfather sold her into the trade. She spent years in Belarus with a sadistic pimp who beat her regularly. When the opportunity came, she didn't hesitate to slit his throat and run away. She felt no remorse so when she needed to make money, she learned to kill and became very good at it... became the best in the world."

"That's not something I'd brag about," Mack said.

"In any case, what she saw with Alexa and Fiona must have gotten to her. We'll see. That being said, it's all upside with her and she's already helping. J Otis ordered Pogladek killed. She and Gregorz staged his murder. Gregorz and his family are safely on their way to Miami with new identities. J Otis thinks he has his hired gun back."

"J Otis is back in Moscow?"

Swerdlov nodded. "We found the silver Mercedes in Belfast near the port, parked suspiciously close to a disgraced pill-dispensing doctor's house. He admitted treating J Otis for bullet wounds in his shoulder and thigh. Later, J Otis either slipped out of the country on a private plane or by ship. Either way, he's back and being protected in Moscow. Becca is working to get him out of the country. That's when we nab him."

"I'm still not convinced she can be trusted," Mack added. "She enjoys killing too much."

Gunn opened his palms and said, "She and I have an ironclad, non-negotiable agreement."

Mack didn't need to ask. He knew what that meant.

§

ABOUT THE AUTHOR

Before turning to writing, Johnny Mee was a banker, restaurant owner, defense industry analyst and a band manager. His first job was hustling programs and scorecards at Minnesota Twins baseball games when he was 12 years old.

Johnny is the author of 5 other Billy Mack Thrillers.

Check out his web site at www.johnnynovels.com

CPSIA information can be obtained
at www.ICGtesting.com
Printed in the USA
BVHW042139061022
648909BV00009B/41

9 781095 591871